GOD'S OWN COUNTRY

Bart Wolffe

ISBN 978-1-291-65227-7
First Edition from "A Twist of Tales"
Second Printing 2009

“Kare haagari ari kare”

(The past does not remain the past)
- Shona Proverb

A thousand feet up, the large black eagle tilted its head arrogantly. With a flick of pinions, the bird caught the thermal and played it like an ascending scale, circling ever higher.

Scientific men who think of the flight of birds as a mere part of their functional nature have obviously never watched an eagle at play. This bird would stoop, locked into its mating dance, high above the mountain, its call penetrating the wind like a sword, and then flick its wings to soar swooping with the ease only super heroes could dream of.

Having reached its zenith, the bird tilted its head once more and with a telescopic eye, penetrated the horizon down below for signs of life and movement. Indeed, movement there was, from the lonely, little red sports car that caressed the curves of the dusty Nyanga mountain road. The car wove towards the escarpment overlooking the green and stream-ribboned valley where the farm nestled, a toy-town dream in miniature far below.

In the car, the passenger, a young woman, turned and brushed her hair back through manicured nails.

“Do you think he’ll sell?”

Adjusting his shoulders back into the seat, the husband grunted his assurance.

“If the price is right, the old bugger will only be too glad to get rid of the farm. I mean, apparently, he lives there alone."

"Uh-huh," his wife responded and slid down a few more inches into her reverie, closing her eyes with a smile twitching about the edges of her lips. The wind whistled around her, blowing her hair in a cloud of silk about her ears.

They reached the crest of the hill and the junction of the valley road where the painted plough-disc signs of homesteads spelt out the names of the local populace ... "The Heath" - D. Small, "Orchard Brook" - Joy & George Rowse, "High Country" - The Van Vurens.

High Country was their intended destination. Like so many city dwellers seeking escape from the rat-race, the Grahams were looking to buy the small farm as a retreat. In this scenic world, most of the inhabitants were actually weekend visitors, driving up from Harare on school holidays with their children or on holiday weekends such as Easter, Independence or Christmas. The regulars were all retired, using the mountain setting to idle their days in trout fishing and fruit growing, or the occasional, round of golf and given to the odd spell of hobby painting and bottling of home made Mother-Trot's Mountain Raspberry Jam and apple blossom honey. The community had its own library, its own church, its own postmaster and policeman as well as its own little old ladies' tea parties, pattern making sessions and gossip gatherings. The main thing was that here, they would all be safe and untouched by the news of the outside world, only having to tune to BBC World Service at six for the news of Wimbledon or Wall Street. This was a blue-print for paradise, a pattern for heaven on earth and earned Nyanga the rather presumptuous title of God's own country.

But more importantly, everyone believed in it. As did the prospective purchasers of paradise; the Grahams. - After a few minutes their car arrived at the white pillars announcing the driveway to High Country. Graham slowed the car down into second gear and turned in. The driveway was full of corrugations and potholes.

"Damn," he muttered. "You need a bloody four-wheel drive to get to this place!"

The wife, woken from her reverie by the jolting of the little car, gasped as she saw the farmhouse come into view.

"Oh, Honey, it's so pretty, just like a real Cape cottage, gables and all."

Ignoring his wife's enthusiasm, Graham continued with his concern for the wretchedness of the driveway.

"We'll have to get the road fixed when - if - we buy the damn place. That's our first priority!"

Turning past an outhouse, Graham pulled to a stop in front of the entrance. A bed of lupines seemed to have run riot in mauves and pinks outside the front door. Hawthorn hedging sprawled unkempt and uncut, burdened with berries along the side of the garden. Despite the unruly impression, the cottage had a certain fairy tale appearance with its little plantation of pines overshadowing the back of the house, silhouetting the wood smoke that rose into the already sweet mountain air.

"It's lovely darling, I want it already! Oh, I do hope he'll sell."

Graham led his wife by the hand to the front porch and clacked the old doorknocker twice. An omen of death, on the door frame of the cottage, a leopard skull hung menacingly. No reply. This time he rapped hard on the wood with his knuckles.

For a while the Grahams stood looking at each other. Nervously, the wife proffered;

"What if he's not...?"

Just at that moment, the door opened to reveal the apparition of an old white man with tobacco-stained teeth and beard, shadows deep and grey in the bags under his eyes. A cold chill swept into Mrs. Graham's ample helvey-knit bosom as a distinctly Vreistaat accent boomed out scowlingly at her.

"Ya? - what do you want?"

Undaunted by the initial frigidity of the homesteader, Graham spoke up, hand outstretched in welcome.

"Mr Van Vuren I presume, I'm Jonathan Graham."

"You presume too much!" came back the reply, the door already being shoved in the visitors' faces.

Graham was not being put off. His outstretched hand held the door ajar while he blurted out an apology.

"Sorry to trouble you Mr. Van Vuren. We're just up for the weekend"

"So?" - One word punched out, disinterestedly.

Anne Graham came to the rescue with a smile designed to make peace.

"It's beautiful up here, I mean, isn't it?"

Van Vuren, obviously not into social etiquette, retorted; "Is it?"

Again, hesitation as Graham found himself at a loss for words. But he was not going to give up, especially now that the rebuff had come from an Afrikaner, the one species on earth that Graham with his blue colonial blood could not abide. And even more so, being a salesman divested of a certain degree of sensitivity, here was a sales pitch that demanded attention, even if just to get a look at the place.

"Look, Van Vuren, we were just trying to be neighbourly." Before Van Vuren could interrupt, Graham continued pointedly;

"My wife, Anne and I, we're only up here for the weekend. We're staying at Troutbeck actually. We saw your place from the hilltop and found it an enchanting sight, so we thought we'd drop in and just say hello."

"Is that so?" Van Vuren retorted. "How did you know my name?"

"Fellow by the name of De Villiers, I think it was. Your name was also on the sign. Well, actually, my wife and I were thinking of buying a holiday cottage, a sort of retreat - you know, escape from the city, summer house sort of thing."

Realising he hadn't put himself across too clearly, Graham turned by way of explanation;

"I'm in the estate agency game myself. Thought it would be a good investment. You see, I have some money saved, quite a bit, actually. As you are obviously an authority on the district, perhaps you could advise us?"

Van Vuren shifted uneasily. He was not in the habit of welcoming strangers on his turf. Graham's wife, Anne, was in the meantime, trying to poke her head around Van Vuren's shoulders to catch a glimpse of the interior. Van Vuren was not insensitive to her intrusion, albeit her just looking, and his eyes darted furtively back and forwards between the two invaders of his sanctuary. In the few seconds that it took for

Anne Graham to accommodate an image of the interior, she took in a variety of bric-a-brac in the form of African curios, masks and carvings, Several soapstone statuettes stood on odd shelves and tables, grotesquely squeezed from the stone it seemed ... knobkerries on one wall and ... her eyes froze in mid-glance; she was confronted by the most extraordinarily beautiful painting of a young girl against a background of mountains, the child flaxen and possessing an air of the very scenery in her, yes, as if the mountains had been made to frame this young beauty with their surrounding crown.
Involuntarily, Anne Graham blurted out;

"What a beautiful painting!"

Van Vuren stodgily blocked her view by shifting his foot to one side. Graham in the meanwhile continued with his sales pitch.

"Actually, someone suggested you might be interested in selling up."

As if receiving a sudden blow below the belt, Van Vuren's face flushed and sagged all at once. He recovered himself and asked abruptly;

"Who?'

"Someone at the hotel. Someone we met while we were having..."

Anne Graham, fascinated by the painting, interrupted her husband to push past Van Vuren impulsively, with a lack of logic that it so often takes to break the ice between people on meeting for the first time.

"Mr Van Vuren, that is such a beautiful picture and what a lovely, lovely child!"

This gesture put Van Vuren at a complete loss. What made it worse was the fact that the wife had already maneuvered herself half-way past him to stare up at the painting on the wall with a look of absolute adoration. With a mumbling gesture to Graham, Van Vuren stuttered an apology.

"Please ... I'm sorry, it's just that I'm not exactly used to having visitors, not since - "

Van curtailed his sentence with a forced and strange laugh and motioned the husband inside the house.

The interior of the farmhouse was typically settler-styled. In the one corner, an old Victorian settee. Next to it, a tall standard lamp. A heavy mahogany sideboard accompanying an equally solid dining-room table and chairs. Two high-backed arm chairs and shotgun over the fireplace near a brass mirror and coal scuttle and bellows completed the picture but for the assortment of odd African artifacts and several paintings depicting stonework ruins with bright slashes of flowering, red aloes rough-hewn amongst greenery and tangles of stems and roots. And of course, the painting of the young girl, gazing angelically on any visitor that happened to come into the house.

"I'm sorry," re-iterated Van Vuren. "Please, do have a seat."

"Quite alright old boy. Perhaps we should have let you know that we intended to come and visit. I suppose we could have phoned, but that forestry fellow, De Villiers or whoever, said you would be in anyway. Apparently, you don't mix much with the community."

Graham snorted and gave a shrug and nonchalant laugh as he walked over and subsided into one of the armchairs. His wife, instead of sitting, went across to the painting of the young girl and stood for several moments admiring it, then brushed her fingertips across the surface as if trying to capture something of the texture of the child's long, gold hair.

"She is lovely. - Relative of yours?"

Embarrassed, Van Vuren lowered his eyes and spoke two words.

"My daughter."

"She must be a very beautiful woman by now. Does she visit you often?" This said with a woman's softness for something familiar and precious. Yet despite Anne Graham's touch of interest, Van Vuren acted as though he hadn't heard. In fact, he walked across to the bay window and gazed out onto the panorama of the mountains in silence.

Graham, conceding that his wife had perhaps a better approach then his own initial gambit, picked up a fly whisk made from an animal's tail and proceeded to flick it up and down in the palm of his hand as he said;

"Must have a very lucky husband, what?"

Slowly, Van Vuren turned towards Graham and spoke so quietly, almost as if he didn't have the breath to comment;

"She's gone."

Not understanding, Graham continued.

"Well, daddy's little girl has to grow up eventually, I suppose, old boy. Whatever, you must be very proud of her - she living in South Africa eh?"

Van Vuren suddenly found himself infuriated by Graham's tone and barked at him:

"I said she's gone! - Dead. -Don't you understand?"

Attempting to recover from his faux-pas, the

husband got up and wandered over to the mantelpiece, brushing the fly whisk lightly over the face of a traditional mask.

"I say, you seem to be rather fond of Africa, all these bits and pieces."

"They were my wife's," Van mumbled. "She found it fascinating."

Anne Graham looked round from the picture.

"Your wife?"

"She's gone. I mean she's ... dead."

"I'm so sorry," proffered Anne Graham.

With a slightly sour turn of voice, Van spoke;

"Well, you didn't exactly know her. But I'm very sorry too."

"It must be very lonely up here by yourself, Mr Van Vuren," Anne added sincerely. "Really, you should get away, go and meet people, move to Harare, perhaps, or Mutare."

"This is my home; I belong here." Van answered inaudibly.

The conversation was proving heavy going and in an attempt to change the subject, Jonathon Graham put down the fly whisk and picked up a small leather pouch on a thong, began fingering it. Holding it out towards his host, he enquired.

"What's in it?"

"I've never opened it. I..."

"Probably some hocus-pocus bits and pieces," Graham laughed, a vain attempt at humour in the face of adversity. Van Vuren swallowed visibly.

"Traditional medicine, I suppose."

Looking up at Van querulously, Graham enquired in earnest.

"You believe that nonsense?"

"It's not nonsense!" shot back the reply.

"Come on old boy, you can't be truly serious. Abracadabra and all that?"

For some reason, this conversation seemed to upset the host more than the mention of his deceased family. He made a move towards the fireplace, stopped, turned back to Graham.

"Listen, Mr Graham, you don't know a thing about it. I must ask you to leave my house. Now." - This last word punched out with the flatness of cold steel.

Jonathon Graham was not to be deterred by such a display of hostility and indignantly retorted.

"I'm sorry that we seem to have offended you by our attempt to show you some degree of civility. I mean, we were just trying to be sociable, you know. Everyone is entitled to believe what they want to, superstitions or whatever, I suppose." With a snort, he threw down the pouch onto the table and stretched out his hand to his wife.

"Come on Anne, we're leaving."

In an instant, Van Vuren had stepped across to the fireplace and removed the shotgun. With a single breaking action, he inserted two SSG cartridges from the mantelpiece and as he snapped it shut, wheeled on the incredulous couple. The Grahams heard the pent-up scream of a madman unleash itself from deep in Van Vuren's subconscious.

"You're a bloody fool! - You don't know a bloody thing I'll show you!"

Graham's face sagged as his wife reached out and squeezed her nails into his arm in terror. He made a move towards Van Vuren, unable to believe this was really happening.

"Come on old fellow, put it down."

Van screamed hysterically;

"Get back!"

The gun swung left and right over the captive couple. Van's eyes seemed to pulse with a fear that caused his throat to contract. His eyes darted round the room, to the door, back to the captive Grahams.

"Very well, you wanted to poke your rich little noses into somebody else's business - OK!"

Thrusting the barrel of the shotgun into the stomach of the frightened husband he bellowed;

"SIT!" He repeated the same action to the wife. "SIT, I SAID!"

Unable to do anything but obey, the Grahams slumped into the settee in a stupor of fear. Van covered them hysterically with the gun, swinging the barrel back and forth, not letting himself untense for even a moment. His eyes never left the husband while he backed towards the sideboard. For some moments, he stood there as if on the edge of an act that had no stopping. Then, with his one hand, he reached into the sideboard and removed a bottle of brandy. Methodically, he placed the bottle on top of the sideboard, then reached in again to produce a glass. His eyes and the aim of the barrels never withdrew from his hostages, the Grahams.

- Deftly, his left hand unscrewed the top of the brandy. He poured a full glass. Drank, slowly. Then seemed after an age to relax somewhat. Replacing the glass on the sideboard, Van started to speak.

"You think I'm out of my head."

For a moment, he seemed to consider the implications of his own question.

"Well, no, not really." Another slug of the raw spirit and he continued.

"What do you know, Graham, about the Manica people, their beliefs, their gods, their legends. - I'll tell you what you know man - nothing!"

With his captive audience pinned before his eyes, unflinching and fixed as the steel of his weapon, Van Vuren began speaking slowly, purposefully, with a strange distance in his speech as if his mind was coming from a very far and unknown country, a haunted place inhabited by unknown ghosts.

"About twenty-five years ago, I arrived in this country. I came directly to Nyanga, because it was a place free of the crowds of city scum like you. Yes, My God, it was a place to be settled. A place where a man could make a future with his own two hands... I came and built a farm. - I started ranching sheep. Ya, I was one of the first. Of course, it wasn't easy. We had our problems. Was never enough money for what we needed. But I was strong. I had two good hands. Disease, leopards, it didn't matter. Nothing and no-one was going to make me move. This was God's own country, or so I thought. Ya, I was young and here to stay."

For a moment, Van's eyes turned misty. Then hard back on the captive Grahams.

"Damn it! I thought I had everything in control. I didn't want any help. I didn't need anything. Until - until Jenny came."

In his mind's eye, Van Vuren was sitting in the pub at Troutbeck surrounded by the laughter of strong, young men's voices. The pub was warm and friendly, the wood fire cracking in the hearth. A smell of pipe tobacco and rain on woollen jerseys filled the room. And the voices laughing amidst the trophy mounts of trout and antelope heads on the walls.

Around a table near the door, a crowd of young men stood. Van was watching the scene from his bar stool. On the table was a book, a fisherman's log. Towering above the table, a big, bluff man with a military moustache finished writing and then, rather like a preacher from a pulpit, held the "bible" up looking around with drunken benevolence on his flock. Looking down, he began to read from the fisherman's log.

"Today's catch. One fisherman. Caught dead drunk by A. Trout. Weight with beer, two hundred and thirteen pounds. Type of fly - open!"

The big man burst into an infectious roar of laughter joined by his fan club. Van called out from his seat by the bar;

"Better make sure the colonel doesn't recognise your handwriting man. You'll be banned from fishing for the next ten seasons."

More laughter as the good humour of the pub's snuggery worked its spell. As abruptly as the laughter began, it was cut short by the entrance of a young woman in a tweed skirt with a blond halo of hair arriving with the unexpected visitation of an angel in the midst of an unholy gathering. For some moments, the girl in her mid-twenties gazed at the man and the men, middlingly sobered, gazed back at her. Then through the smoky haze, her voice rang out like crystal, English crystal.

"Excuse me, can any of you men direct me to a slave pit?"

The silence continued to prevail while every man's

eyes scanned the long legs and slim ankles. They noted simultaneously the startlingly blue eyes enhancing the innocence of the woman's appearance in their midst. This innocence was soon to be shattered by the joker. "A slave pit? - Why, do you want to buy a slave?" Turning to the barman, the joker called out: "Solomon, are any of your brothers for sale?"

Once again laughter crescendoed in the male domain. In the doorway, the woman blushed visibly and was about to turn and leave the lion's den when Van stepped off his stool and approached her, taking hold of her arm.

"Well, as a matter of fact Miss, I have a very nice one on my farm. It's a few minutes drive up the road."

For a moment the woman seemed hesitant. Then, abruptly, she thrust out her hand to Van.

"Jenny Thompson. Very pleased to make your acquaintance."

By way of explanation she proffered;

"I'm an artist, just visiting. I was hoping to sketch one of the slave pits in the area and any other ruins you might happen to know of. It's for my collection of studies for my Masters degree in Fine Art."

"You out from University in Britain then?" Van responded weakly.

"Call me Jenny," she smiled winningly. Van was smitten, totally, as were all the men in the room.

"Ya Jenny," Van savoured her name. "And you call me Van."

A snigger from the joker in the background; "Fast work, Van my man!"

"And you are?" Jenny enquired of him, winning him over completely, just as butter melts to warmth.

"Uh, it's Dawie Ma'am," came the humble reply, the big man removing his hat for the first time in the pub in awesome deference to beauty.

"Well, if Van doesn't mind, you gentlemen will excuse us. I'd like to see that slave pit on his farm that he promised."

Jenny smiled at the men and took her leave, Van hesitantly poised at his safe stool.

"What are you waiting for? Drink up and go, man!" Dawie prompted the young Van Vuren. Van tilted his beer glass once -and having finished the contents, left to the sound of cat calls and wolf whistles following behind. Summoning up his lost empire, Dawie announced;

"Bet you he tells her the one about the ghosts that come out of the stones at night!"

A titter of laughter returns to the tribe of men affirmatively clutching glasses inside the Troutbeck bar and the incident was forgotten as the mountain mists rolled on.

That first afternoon cast shadows across the land, shadows long as memory. Beside a quiet stream that ran down into a bracken covered valley, Van stopped his truck. Jumping out, he ran round to the passenger door and playing the chivalrous knight, opened it for his lady to dismount. And dismount she did. Her long leg descended slenderly from beneath the tweed skirt in what seemed to Van, the art of slow motion mesmerism. It was followed by Jenny herself.

"Where did you say the slave pit was Van?" Asked Jenny.

"Just across the stream, over there. You can see the top of the stones above the grass, near that fig tree." - Van pointed to where an old African fig sprouted and entwined itself through a low wall of moss and lichen covered stone. Taking her hand, he led Jenny across the stepping stones in the stream and over to the ruins.

The slave pit was a circular affair some ten yards in diameter; about three feet of walling protruded above the ground and on the far side, the old fig tree malevolently twisted its snake-like roots up into a grotesque torso blotched with rotting and midge-bitten fruit. A few yards before the actual wall, a tunnel suddenly dipped into the earth, leading to the underground enclosure. Indeed, the slave pit was so named for its pit or centre lay underground. It was open to the sky above and accessible only by means of the narrow entrance and underground passage which a child of five might be able to enter upright, but any adult would need to stoop and crawl through to enter.

Van took Jenny's hand again and led her in to the stone mouth. Behind him, her voice echoed as if in a catacomb.

"Did they really keep slaves in here?"

Van's voice carried back over his shoulder to her.

"They say you can still hear them moan in their chains at night."

Feeling Jenny's had tightened her grip, he assured her with a laugh.

"Actually, it's the wind. We call it the Nyanga wind, the one with the lonely tongue. It's quite something in these hills. The slave pits were probably to protect livestock from the leopards in these mountains, really."

On stepping into the interior of the slave pit, one could indeed hear the wind as it picked its whining, whispering way through the cracks and cavities of stone and the leafy fig tree overhead. - A lizard, on seeing the couple enter, flicked its head up and down and darted for cover to peer out at them between the blocks of stone and old man's beard that hung green and tangled down the inside wall from the fig's grey roots.

In silence they stood, still holding hands, listening to the list and whine of the wind as it played round the ruin, changing direction, changing source every few seconds. Other than the wind, silence reigned in their underground enclosure, with just the sky above and the leafy canopy of green. It was as if the world outside has ceased to exist.

"It's really exciting. Sort of has a feel about it, as if ancient beings were watching us", Jenny said in hushed and muted tones, as if out of respect for the dead. Releasing Van's hand, she withdrew a few charcoals from her carry bag and took out her sketch pad which she opened on her lap as she sat on a fallen block of stone. Deliberately and firmly, she began to draw. Van watched her, enraptured by the methodical strokes that soon took shape as block on block, she built the wall around her, shading it simultaneously with brooding cracks suggesting hidden things.

Taking his pipe out of his pocket, Van started to stoke it up and commented to her;

"That's quite a talent you've got there, Miss Thompson."

Over her shoulder, Jenny cast an approving glance and smiled at the way Van had offered his praise. The smell of pipe tobacco mingled with the scent of humus and mulch underfoot, bringing a sense of a world both ancient and yet totally present, immediately right there, where they shared this ground of being. Van kicked into a pile of leave mould to reveal a scuttling beetle and millipede that immediately and defensively knotted itself into a tight ball.

"Please don't hang around for me," Jenny spoke. "I'll walk up to the house and join you for a cup of tea later. I really prefer to sketch without someone watching me." - Again, she smiled winningly at Van.

"Agh, it's alright. I'm sure you're like me when you do something seriously, you know, pulling faces to yourself and all that," laughed Van. But secretly, he felt rejected by Jenny's not wanting him around to act out the role of guardian in this alien place.

"No, really Van, don't wait. I'd like to walk back later for the exercise, anyway." Again, that smile.

Taking his pipe out of his mouth, Van grunted, lest he appear too interested;

"Well alright, I'll go now. But you come up for some tea when you've finished. And do be careful of snakes."

A pause as Van waited for confirmation from Jenny who was already deeply engrossed in the atmosphere of her study.

"See you later then," Van said, trying not to betray his disappointment that a work of art could take apparent priority over his presence. Jenny just nodded what was understood as agreement to the tea offer, so Van stooped and exited from the pit.

As the sound of the bakkie engine coughed into life, Jenny looked up a moment. Resting her hand underneath her chin she looked deeply engrossed in the privacy of her thoughts. Then she turned back to the task at hand, taking out some pastels to fill in hints of moss and lichen. Time was lost and as the shadows began to brood, Jenny was soon on her third attempt at capturing an atmosphere that could only be described truly in the being there, alone with the stones of history, mysterious and made more so by the wind's longing tongue.

Reaching down for a dark green, she looked up the twisted torso of the fig tree until her eye rested amidst the thick foliage at the top. Involuntarily, she let out a gasp. For the greenery parted to reveal an old black man, bare from the midriff up, wearing a sort of monkey-skin skirt, who proceeded to squat, arms crossed, on the ledge and stare down at Jenny as if she were his prisoner in the pit. But it was his face that drew Jenny's eye, for he began to rock back and forth on his haunches, laughing silently with mouth agape, toothlessly, his tongue rolling in and out in a mockery of silence. Absolutely no sound came from him to the accompaniment of her beating heart. For several seconds, Jenny froze, rooted there by this primitive apparition, the pink cavern with its toothless gums rocking away in silent laughter. Then quite suddenly and without forewarning, the old man jumped off the wall backwards and out of sight. Alarmed, Jenny called out;

"Who's there - what do you want?" - Her voice echoed round the stone walls bouncing back accusingly at her. In fright, she dropped the pad and pastels from her hand and stumbled towards the tunnel exit. Hurrying through, she scraped herself on the cold stone and gasped as she stepped out into the late sunlight. She looked around to spot her voyeur but there was no sign of the old fellow. Hesitantly,

Jenny began to circumvent the periphery of the wall expecting to come face to face with him at any moment. Suddenly, a spring-hare leapt up from the undergrowth and bounded away from almost underfoot and caused Jenny to scream in fright. Her heart now pounded like thunder inside. She found herself back at the tunnel entrance from the other side without having met any trace or sign of the old man. Where had he gone? Shivering, she stepped into the tunnel expecting to come face to face with him at any moment. Nothing. No-one. Just the emptiness of the wind. Gathering her belongings hurriedly, Jenny exited from the pit and began the climb for the farmhouse, for the experience had taken away any further desire to sketch, that day anyway. In fact, why had she been so casual as not to allow Van to keep her company when he had been so polite and helpful in the first place?

Back in the farmhouse lounge, the young Van Vuren was reading a copy of the Rhodesian Farmer of May, 1955. A record year for tobacco prices was promised. - Perhaps he should have been in tobacco, Van thought. Not pioneering the sheep industry in the mountains where leopards and locals interfered with every attempt he made to build up his best breeding stock. The cold snap had already killed several lambs this year.

He crossed his legs and took a puff from his cold pipe. Wondered how Jenny was doing with her sketching. At his feet, the ridgeback stretched out a hind leg and started scratching behind his ear.

"Stop it boy!" Van commanded, reaching down and giving the hound a tap on his nose. Just then, the dog's ears pricked up as if hearing something. It let out a slight yelp, a sort of half-bark and jumped to its feet, heading for the door. Van looked up to see the door open and a disheveled and breathless Jenny Thompson appear in the doorway. A scratch showed redly on her knee and she looked pale and frightened.

"Good God Jenny!" Van started. "What happened? - You look like you've seen a ghost!"

Getting to his feet, Van stepped over to Jenny and tried to lead her by the arm to a chair. But Jenny just avoided his grasp and moved across to the bay window to look out at the gathering gloom on the mountains.

"Perhaps I have Van. Perhaps that is just what I did see... a ghost!"

Van regarded Jenny curiously. He was about to add that he shouldn't have left her alone but thought better of it when Jenny turned to him and asked;

"Tell me Van, do you know anything about an old African with the teeth missing in the front of his mouth?"

Van pricked up abruptly, taking a particular interest in what Jenny just said.

"This old man, with the missing teeth - when you saw him, did he say anything?"

"You know him then," Jenny remarked, looking directly into Van's flinching gaze.

In the lounge of the farmhouse cottage, an old and weary Van Vuren stopped in his story for a moment, shifted the shotgun from his right arm to his left and reached for the brandy bottle. After filling his glass with the raw spirit, he drank. He then walked across to the stone fireplace and kicked a log, sending a shower of sparks and dead ash flying.

"Still think I'm crazy, huh?" He accused his audience, the captive Grahams. Walking back to the sideboard, he reached out for the glass and drank again. After a minute's silence, he spoke.

"Jenny hadn't even been here one day and she had seen the silent one."

As if on afterthought, Van walked behind the dining-room table and pulled out a chair, sat, the gun rested pointing at the belly of the captive husband. He looked at Graham and said.

"Pour yourself one if you like. You're going to need it soon."

Graham hesitated and got up. His eyes gave the game away. His intentions took in the gun, the distance between the brandy bottle and Van Vuren. Immediately, with all the instincts of a hunted animal, Van sensed this and barked;

"Don't even think of trying it!"

Van made his point in an eloquent and startling way. He swung the gun towards the kitchen door, single-handed and fired one barrel. The door splintered before their eyes. Van Vuren laughed at the wife's scream of fear.

"On second thoughts, don't bother about the drink. I need it more."

Lifting the bottle, Van refilled his glass and drank again. Wiping away the spill of liquid from his beard and chin onto his shirt.

"Now you know what'll happen to you man, if you think I'm joking."

Graham had slumped back into his seat. As easily as Van had started to laugh, he stopped. His face was dark and glowering.

"When I've finished telling you, perhaps you'll

understand. You might even begin to believe, because you're no longer in control of your world, Graham." Again, Van started laughing as a sudden flash of lightning and a loud peal of thunder from the approaching storm filled the evening sky. From Van's mouth came a strange and haunted moan, as if a man possessed.

"Just like the night it happened. - Rain coming - the storm!"

Anne Graham was scared. Very scared. She reached out her hand to her husband seated rigidly next to her on the settee and whispered under her breath.

"John, I'm frightened!"

Bloodlessly, Jonathon Graham opened his mouth to speak.

"Listen, Van Vuren, we mean you no harm. Please, let us go!"

"NO!" Van screamed at him. "I said you're involved! - Don't you understand what I'm trying to say to you? You opened a door that you shouldn't have, without even knocking, and now you're here and you're involved, whether you like it or not!"

A flash of lightning again in the evening sky followed by a rumble of thunder rolling deep-bellied across the hills.

"Just like the night it happened," Van reiterated. "He's watching us tonight, you know!"

Van seemed to sense that his audience wouldn't flinch. He got up and walked to the window and looked out on the darkening mountains. Turning his back to his audience, he adjusted the gun in the crook of his arm and continued.

"I didn't believe them when they told me about the old fellow. Thought they were crazy. Just like you think I am. But then I saw him, with my own eyes. Yes, there was no escaping my destiny. And Graham, there is no escape for any of us, no escape at all!"

Before Van's eyes, the scene of a mountain road in the moonlight unfurled. Van as a young man on his return from a night at the pub with good friends, lazily ascending the escarpment to the turn-off to his snug and welcoming farm. In the back of the bakkie, Van's dog, the ridgeback, Van's favourite animal on earth.

As the car mounts the top of the rise, the figure of an old man steps into the road to be highlighted suddenly in the glare of the headlamps. The old man's back is towards the approaching vehicle. He makes no sign of stepping out the way. Van jabs the hooter, suddenly jolted out of his semi-drunken and indolent drive home. He jabs at the hooter. - It is as if the man has not heard. In a squeal of brakes, Van pulls to a standstill as the old fellow turned round to face him. In the beam of the vehicle, the old man is laughing. Silently. Laughing from a toothless mouth. Van's dog begins to bark.

Angrily, Van opened the door of the truck and got out to confront the old fellow. When he looked up, there was no trace of him. He had just disappeared to all intents and purpose into the night. A sudden rush of wings made Van instinctively duck his head as a large eagle owl softly passed overhead through the beam of the headlight. Suddenly, Van became aware of the size of the silence around him. The night wind ranging the endless mountains. All around him, the sounds of the dark seemed to begin to swell and fill the air. Down in the valley, the cry of a wild creature as if in pain. In the back of the bakkie, Van's dog began to howl.

"Oh yes, I knew who it was that Jenny had seen. I knew the stories too. Ghost stories and about people vanishing mysteriously and the sighting of the old beggar like a sign of impending fate. But I also knew that this was God's own country. And no superstitions, no black magic or whatever, were going to screw up my life and my future. My future with my new wife."

High up in the Nyanga mountains, the sound of "The Lord is my Shepherd" filtered from the open doors of the tiny chapel that overlooked a green valley with a tiny lake far below. The voices floated out into the mountain air from the Chapel of Our Lady where a wedding was taking place.

"You may kiss the bride now," the old priest smiled with paternal benediction.

A young and beaming Van Vuren lifted the veil from the face of an angel and pressed his lips to hers. From some joker amongst the gathered witnesses came the sound of a slow, low wolf-whistle. Van turned and winked at the big man.

Hand in hand, bride and groom walked out into the morning sunlight. Swallows looped overhead from their nests in the eaves of the little church, so rarely frequented except on Sundays and the occasional special times like this. The priest shook hands with the newly-weds and told them he'd love to join them for a drink but unfortunately he'd have to be getting back to Mutare as he had another engagement. Dawie, the joker strolled over, hands nonchalantly in his pockets and withdrawing them both, proceeded to rub confetti into his friend's hair, mussing it in as if giving it his best shampoo. Then he took the bride aside and gave her the longest kiss he could.

A young Van soon intervened after a few seconds staking claim on his very personal property. Handshakes and congratulations from the few attendant guests.

In his mind's eye, the honeymoon days drifted before Van. (Drifted into happy weeks, months, the first year.)

A young couple picnicking at the Inyangombi mountain pool. A collage of images. They climb dripping naked out of the chill water and he leads her by the hand to a tartan rug spread on the adjacent spit of sand at the water's edge. They collapse laughing onto the rug and kiss. Slowly, Van Vuren starts to twist the ring on her finger round and round in his lips. Parting her fingers, his tongue glides in between the folds of damp skin as he explores the curve of her hand. Slowly, his mouth travels up her arm to her neck, down to her breasts where the beads of water glisten on taut nipples like grapes after the rain. His hand begins to move caressingly across her stomach, into the sleek of her thighs. Together they start moving in rhythm to the sun above, gazing deep as drowning into each other's beauty.

After it is over, Van starts to kiss her again, exploring her mouth like a child rediscovering treasure. She in return, begins to feast back, ever hungry. Laughing and breathless, Van pulls back.

"Happy my sweet?"

The young bride glows at her husband.

"This has to be heaven." - Her fingers play with his lips. "You know, I could die here quite happily!"

"Not yet, not yet please," Van pleads teasingly.

"I just don't want to move. Go on Van, bury me now. I've arrived." Van scoops a handful of sand and pours it over her breasts. She laughs.

"Tell you what Van, I don't want to ever leave these mountains. Oh Van, this is my home. I swear I felt it when I first arrived. Meeting you was the final confirmation."

"OK, you've made your point," Van tries to silence her with a kiss, but like a shy schoolgirl, Jenny breaks away.

"Let me tell you something Mr Van Vuren, before you get too familiar with me." Playing shy, she covers her breasts with her crossed arms as she sits up. "You sir, have an errand to perform. To go to Umtali to do the weekly shopping while I sit and wait for my big white chief to come back to my bed and take me in his arms. I'm not moving, you see."

And with that, Jenny lies back silently and slowly spreads her legs. Opening one eye, she winks at him, teasing, urging him to come back. As Van rolls on top of her, she whispers urgently;

"I don't even want to hear what is happening in the big wide world outside. If World War 3 starts let me be the last to know."

Van smiles back adoringly at his woman, his eyes soft with worship.

"You're just a dreamer, honey. Honestly, I do hope my English princess is not going to die of boredom surrounded by nothing but sheep all day."

Jumping to his feet, Van pulls her up behind him.

"Come on, one more dip before we go home and get

ready for Dawie's."

Like children, they run chasing each other, splashing into the pool. The waterfall drowns their laughter as it tumbles down from underneath the bridge high above. There is no passing traffic. It is paradise. Only the figure of an old man who appears on the parapet, gazing down on them as they continue to splash and chase each other into the water. The old man begins to laugh, silently, watching them all the while. Something makes Jenny stop and look up. Seeing the intruder there, she shakes her husband by the shoulder, pointing. Van follows her gaze to the bridge top where the old man stands. He runs out the water and up the bank screaming.

"Hey you, hey! - What the hell do you want! - Go on, Voetsak you dirty bugger !"

Grinning toothlessly, the old man turns and disappears into the shade of the pine forest by the roadside.

"Who is he really? - Who is the old man, Van?"

Van glanced up from the wheel of the truck for a moment.

"I don't know Jen, my darling. The people in the district look on him as a sign when he appears. They think, or seem to believe that he's a legend, like the spirit of their ancestors, the Midzimu."

"But he just looks like a crazy old beggar to me, dressed in monkey skins and beads. A raggedy old man in fact..." Jenny attempts a laugh.

"Nyanga is the ancestral home," Van continued. "The home of the spirits to the Manica people. Many of them consider it sacred ground. There's even a legend about Nyanga being the place where the doors to paradise are always open. They say you can cross over without even dying. People have been known to just disappear here. I've read many reports of tourists vanishing."

"Well, it's beautiful enough here to be in paradise, perhaps it's not such a bad idea to get lost here, really!" affirmed Jenny.

Van continued.

"Did you know that most of the witchdoctors or Nangas come from this part of the country."

Jenny persisted in trying to accommodate the image of the old man in her mind. Struggling to make sense of the apparition, if indeed, that was what he was.

"Where does he live then? - I mean, he is flesh and blood, isn't he?"

Van turned and smiled assuringly at her.

"There are a lot of caves in the area." He laughed briefly, trying to make light of the subject. "Probably, he throws bones in one of them... Come on honey, this conversation is getting a little heavy. Just forget him Jen. After all, we're going to have ourselves a party at Dawie's tonight."

As they reached the white pillars, Van changed down and turned into the home stretch. It was just at that moment that Jenny leant over and kissed him on the cheek. She then flicked her hair back and whispering in his ear, proceeded to deliver a major piece of information to him as casually as if she was asking him whether he wanted one egg or two for breakfast.

"Van, I'm going to have a baby."

- At this announcement, Van swerved the wheel with surprise. He turned to Jenny and kissed her fully on the lips. For a moment, the truck left the driveway and veered off the road, bouncing up and down. Van began to roar with laughter as he righted the vehicle.

"A little Van huh?! - Jenny, are you sure? - God!" He shouted aloud, out the window. "You hear that you dirty old bugger, we're here to stay. The Van Vurens are the future, not you and your bloody ancestral spooks! Jenny, my darling, we really WILL have ourselves a celebration at Dawie's tonight."

Turning to Van, Jenny smiled at him softly, forgiving the impetuosity of his outburst. Placing her hand on his thigh as they drove into the yard, she gave him a loving squeeze as if to assure them both that everything was perfect and would be, always.

Dawie rose from the head of the table. By this stage of the evening he had already had a few too many to drink. He looked round the table at his dinner guests and focused his eyes on Jenny adoringly. Dressed in a slinky, red and low-cut evening gown, she looked stunning. Licking his lips, Dawie raised his glass and called for a toast.

"Ladies and gentlemen - a toast - to the most extra-extra-ordinary beautiful lady in the red, pity about her husband, oh, and yes, tonight," he hesitated, beaming at Jenny for nearly a full minute while everyone held on bravely for what was to come next.

"Tonight, a special toast to the little Van Vuren to be ... May he, she or it be blessed with both Jenny's beauty and brains!"

A slight laughter, like a wave of embarrassment swept the table. But all round took it in good heart as they rose to drink to Jenny and Van. Dawie's girlfriend, Sheila, a round-faced girl with a pretty, pert smile, looked up at Dawie sadly. In her mind, she dreamed of curly-headed little boys and dolls houses. But something told her that such things would never be. For Dawie was not the marrying kind. He was far too frivolous and besides, too much of a flirt to get serious over any woman. Sheila knew this and smiled wistfully to herself.

In response to Dawie's toast, Van took to the floor, rising to his feet when the cries of "to Jenny, to Van, to the little one" had died down.

"As a true gentleman, may I respond." - He paused in his delivery a moment to let the impact sink in. "To good friends," he raised his glass towards Dawie, continued, "even if they are full of shit!" The table erupted with laughter once again, this time a little more whole-heatedly. Finishing his toast, Van added;

"To the future, for all of us. To God's own country, Inyanga, where we will always belong!" and he drank the remains of his glass.

Everyone rose and joined the toast with a rousing "Hear, hear!" Then, initiated by Dawie, they broke into "For they are jolly good fellows" followed up by "Why was he born so beautiful," especially aimed at Van. Jenny sat blushing slightly at the open admiration that Dawie's eyes were lavishing on her.

After dinner, they all adjourned to the sitting room of the Forestry Commission cottage where Dawie wandered around affably replenishing everyone's drinks. When he got to Jenny, he positively glowed at her.

"C'mon, Jenny my darling, have another drink. Gimme your glass."

"No, really Dawie, I've had my share," she smiled warmly at him.

"C'mon, just one more."

"Thanks Dawie, but no. I don't want the baby to turn into an alcoholic before it's even arrived," she laughed.

The mood around the room was slightly more than mellow. Rather like an over-ripe cheese. Van smiled at Sheila and attempted politeness.

"When's your turn?"

With her pretty and sad smile, Sheila shrugged her shoulders. In another corner, a couple, the Andersons, were involved in one another over the pretence of a coffee table book on trout fishing. Jenny turned to Dawie and endeavoured to engage him in some serious conversation in the hope that he might make some sense after all.

"These people that the newspapers claim have disappeared without trace in the mountains, do you believe it?"

Dawie, spread-eagled in his favourite armchair next to his favourite woman friend, just grunted drunkenly.

"Do you think they've been killed Dawie," Jenny persisted. "Or do you think they've really crossed over to the unknown country, the home of the ancestors like the local people seem to believe?"

Dawie twisted his torso in this chair in an attempt to look more fully into Jenny's eyes.

"Jenny, my darling, you know these blighters. - This is Africa. They keep control by putting the fear of God or ghosts or whatever into you. Some of the old-timers feel that we whites have no right to farm on their ancestral land. So, maybe, they're just trying to scare us away. The boogy-man's gonna come and get you ARRRH!" He launched forward towards Jenny nearly collapsing in a heap on the floor.

"Get serious Dawie!" Jenny pleaded with a laugh, unable to help but find Dawie a total crazy sight, totally uncontrollable in his present state.

"OK Jen, there have been quite a few locals disappearing lately. But maybe they got chewed by a leopard. Or took a walk across into the Portuguese side of the mountains to escape paying for their other wives. I mean, how the hell am I supposed to know?"

Jenny interjected soberly.

"But you LIVE here Dawie. This is your country. - Aren't you in the least bit interested in the lives of the other people than the whites who live here?"

"Of course I am Jenny." Dawie burst into laughter. "That's why I keep a slave. - L 0 V E M 0 R E!!!" he bellowed through to the kitchen.

"Oh, can't you ever be serious?" Jenny sighed exasperatedly.

Lovemore, the domestic, came running barefoot into the lounge. He was dressed in a waiter's uniform topped by a ridiculous purple fez on his head.

"Yes baas?"

"Bring us some coffee with a dash of speed."

"Yes baas, I bring coffee now baas!"

Lovemore hurried out to prepare the coffee. Jenny rose to her feet.

"I'll help Lovemore get the coffee," she volunteered.

"You'll do no such thing!" Dawie bawled. "Bloody hell, he's paid to do what I tell him. That's his job. - If you want to be a servant, do it for your husband, not in my house!"

Dawie's raised voice left a hush about the room. Van rose from his chair.

"For Chrissake Dawie, leave my wife alone! - She happens to come from a civilised country where it's only normal to be courteous and offer to help with something like the coffee!"

In the impending silence of disaster, Jenny rose and left the room upset to "powder her nose". Dawie, like an enraged bull, bellowed back at Van.

"As far as I'm concerned Van Vuren, she can do your washing and ironing and cleaning up after you and bring you your breakfast in bed, but I pay my servant for that job!"

Van coldly told Dawie to go fuck himself. Dawie, more than incensed by the alcohol and the occasion, rose and shouted at Van.

"You tell me to get fucked - in MY house?!"

Lurching over to Van, Dawie used his height and size to give Van a shove backwards over a coffee table upsetting a brandy glass and ashtray.

Springing back, Van swung a right into Dawie's oversized stomach and the big man let out a whoosh as he started to double up. Then straightening up like a jack-knife, Dawie butted Van in the face bringing a spurt of blood from Van's nose.

"STOP IT!" Sheila screamed hysterically. Tom Anderson attempted to play his part in restoring sanity and help break up the scuffle. In the process, a coffee table snapped as the fracas malingered on with the two grown men threatening each other in loud voices.

In the meanwhile, a sniffing and tearful Jenny, on coming out of the bathroom, bumped directly into Lovemore, the domestic, who was waiting for her outside the door. She backed away in fright.

"What do you want Lovemore?" she asked weakly.

Looking around fearfully, the servant whispered urgently at her;

"Madam is having a piccanin!"
Startled, Jenny asked;
"How did you know I was having a baby?"
Lovemore did not reply but rather thrust out a small leather pouch on a thong to Jenny. He then closed her hand about it, blurting a stumbling explanation.
"Madam, this muti is for you and your piccanin. A special nanga give it to me to give you." Darting a look around, he added,
"I must go now, before the baas..."
Too late, for just at that moment, Van walked into the passage and saw Lovemore talking to Jenny. His face became even grimmer on seeing them together.
"Fuck off you!" he shouted at Lovemore. Taking out his handkerchief, Van wiped the blood away from his nose and called after the disappearing servant,
"And you! - You'd better make your baas some strong coffee. He needs it!"
Jenny was about to slip the pouch into her handbag unnoticed by Van. But Van gave her no chance.
"What were you doing talking to that man?" he asked of her. "Nothing. He just wanted to see if I was alright," Jenny lied.
"Then what was that you were putting in your bag?"
"Just my tissue, from wiping my face," Jenny lied again.
Van took hold of Jenny's hand and led her to the back door of the house.
"We're getting out of here, now," he stated without apology.
As the bakkie throbbed into life, Lovemore watched through the curtains of the kitchen window. The

headlamps in the back yard crossed the wall and illuminated the servant's face for a moment. He pulled away from the window and the sound of the engine faded as the truck disappeared into the night.

Silence prevailed at the breakfast table the following morning. Jenny refused to meet Van's gaze. She toyed with her boiled egg without appetite. Over a cup of coffee, Van continued to look at Jenny. Then he spoke.

"I'm sorry about last night. I guess we all had a bit too much to drink and emotions were running a bit high."

A pause from Van as he waited for a response from his wife. When she didn't comment, he repeated,

"I said I was sorry."

Jenny's eyes darted up to meet her husband's. There was fire in her look.

"We all had a bit much to drink; speak for yourself Van!"

Suddenly, Jenny broke down and started weeping openly. Van was distraught as he felt himself surely to blame. The whole scene the night before had indeed been too emotional, and although the episode had been blown out of proportion by the alcohol, a lot of undercurrents including the news of the baby and the meeting with the sight of the old man earlier in the day had all gone to precipitating the incident. But, perhaps even more so, Dawie's obvious flirtation with his wife had put Van on the defense. Van got up and walked round the table to comfort Jenny.

"Hush my darling, it won't happen again. I'll go round to Dawie later and apologise for my behaviour. - Please Jenny, I'm sorry ... Alright?"

"Van," Jenny pleaded, softening, "I don't really

blame you. It's just that - "

"Yes, go on..." Van prompted.

"It's just that, I don't know - things seem to have changed. Van, I'm frightened!" - More tears from his wife as Van puts his arms around her to comfort and stem the sobs, holding her tightly with the pain inside him.

"How do you mean things have changed?"

"Well, I thought I was happy in this country, Van. Now I'm not so certain. Oh, it's not you I'm unhappy with Van, it's more me. I just don't feel like I belong. As if I have no right to be here."

"What do you mean not belong?" Van asked uncertainly, the spectre of the unknown fear in Jenny tearing her away from his closest sharing heart.

"I can't explain it - it's just that I'm frightened."

"Look, don't worry honey. Everything will work out fine. I promise you. Soon the baby will be here and you won't even have time to paint with all the nappy changes." Van summoned together a little laugh. Jenny brightened somewhat, managing to look up at him with a smile. She sniffed and Van reached down brushing away a tear. He then leant over and tenderly kissed her on the forehead.

"I'm sorry Van. I'm just over-reacting." Suddenly, she smiled, taking his hand, looked up at him and changed the subject.

"Van you don't mind if I go up to the ruins of the old fort today, do you? - I just want to spend a little time alone so I can sort out my thoughts. I'll take some paints and sandwiches and coffee in the thermos."

Van appeared a little hesitant. When he considered Jenny's request, on the surface, there was nothing wrong with her wanting to spend time doing a bit of art, but her not wanting to share her innermost battle and thoughts with him then and there was what really bothered him. Somehow, he felt excluded from the reckoning, unsure even as to what the outcome of her love was. It was this insecurity that truly disturbed him. Nevertheless, he smiled at her as he spoke.

"Well, I suppose that's ok. But please be careful though. That's our baby in there and you're my woman and I don't want anything to happen to either of you, see?"

Squeezing his hand, Jenny got up from the table.

"Don't be so negative Van. I'll be extra careful not to fall or anything stupid, I promise. I'll just make some sandwiches and coffee and I'll be gone. I'll see you about tea time this afternoon." As if she read his insecurity, she continued, "I do love you Van Vuren. I could never do without you - don't ever forget that." Reaching up on tiptoe, she planted a kiss on Van's nose. Then like a little girl, she broke free from him and ran through to the kitchen.

The morning sun slanted on the face of the hill where Jenny at the wheel of the pick-up changed gear as she negotiated the strip road winding along to the old fort. The road, a mere track, wove between thrusting granite boulders that jutted out of the heath and bracken. The wind whistled noisily through the cab window. Jenny was in good spirits and in the back of the truck, the ridgeback hung his large jowls over the side, slobbering saliva noisily and happily. At a particularly rough corner where the road snaked between boulders. Jenny slowed right down, negotiating it bumpily. Through the windscreen, she saw the black eagle tilt in the wind and glide out of sight beyond the lie of the land.

As she neared the lower terraces of the ruins, lush, bright-red aloes breached their poker heads out of the stonework and nodded sagely, eagerly in the wind. Jenny sighed with contentment, for indeed, it was a glorious day with the surrounding sweep of mountain scenery in the fresh morning air. And the day was all hers.

Parking the vehicle beside a low stone wall, Jenny got out with her sketch pad, her basket of paints and a canvas, leaving her lunch on the seat inside the cab. She did not bother to lock up; there would be nobody about. The dog bounded along beside her playfully, as Jenny walked over to the edge of the hill and climbed on top of a boulder that gave her a bird's eye view of the valley below. The dog barked as it tried to climb onto the rock beside her, jumping up and down at her feet. Jenny laughed, releasing her tension into the wind, the sun's kiss warm upon her cheek. Two swallows looped and played in the air currents overhead, swooping and diving with their sharp squeaks of apparent delight. Then, scrambling over the stones, she made her way towards the main enclosure of the fort where the highest of the walls were standing. As she scrambled over a broken parapet, she dislodged a stone block revealing a startled lizard. It was an armadillo lizard that looked just like a miniature crocodilian with its armour plating. It darted for cover over the far edge of the stonework. Jenny laughed to herself. On reaching a high-standing portion of walling, she backed away from it posing her hands on her hips and surveying it for its intrinsic artistic merit. - Yes. At almost right angles, a smaller wall broke away to her left. In the apex or corner of the join, a double-headed aloe flowered brightly like a gaudy sentinel on the lookout, its orange and red head slashed against the blue dome of the sky and the grey stone of the fort. There was definitely something archetypal about the look of this corner of the old fortifications. Jenny approved and felt the painting starting to stir under her hand.

Seating herself on a lichen clad rock, finding it comfortable, she proceeded to take out the tools of her talent from the wicker basket at her feet. First she withdrew paints and brushes. Then a rag. Some turpentine followed in a jam jar she had brought which she placed beside her on the ground, on her right. She took out a wooden board that served as a palette and started to mix her colours. With the canvas balanced on her knees and a rock in front, Jenny outlined the shape of the painting to come. Her technique was bold and clean and with the ease of a plasterer, she sculpted the stones from the blue surround of sky on the canvas in front of her. She noted a lizard of the same kind as she had surprised earlier poking its head out of the cracks and peering intently at her. Just then, Butch, the ridgeback, started to growl with hackles raised. Jenny looked up and found herself looking into the face of the old man some yards away behind a far wall. He was grinning at her toothlessly. She did not feel unduly troubled by his appearance however. It was too sunny and beautiful a day to let anxiety come clouding in. She just stared back at him until he disappeared behind some of the stone walling. Quietly, Jenny laid down her canvas and placed the brush into the turpentine.

She got up and began to walk towards where she had seen him vanish from view. Getting to the broken edge of the wall, she put her hand onto the ledge and she scrambled through the gap. As she emerged out the other side, a family of guinea fowl flew up from the grass in noisy consternation shaking their wings in a rattle of stiff feathers and giving Jenny a start. Yet there was no sight of the old guy. He's probably wandered off on his merry, mad way down the hill, Jenny thought. Before walking back to her unfinished canvas, Jenny stooped to pick up a dark feather with white polka-like dots over it, a guinea fowl feather dropped by one of the birds she had just disturbed.

Dropping the feather into her basket, she returned to the task at hand and was soon engrossed again in her labour. She felt she was quite successful in capturing the sweeping arms of the aloe lifted to the sky in praise and she sat back to admire the glistening achievement. Then she started to fill in the contrasting shadows that needed enhancing in the mottled stonework. Just then, she felt a very real shadow pass across her face, a shadow that by its unexpected nature felt much colder and darker than any she had drawn. With a shock, she looked up to see the old man laughing silently a few feet away, staring at her, rocking on his feet, back and forth, back and forth.

"Have you never seen someone paint before?" Jenny asked aloud.

Still, he continued to rock with silent laughter as if not understanding.

"What do you want of me?" Jenny enquired loudly.

The old man looked at Jenny for a moment, looked at the canvas, then back at Jenny once again. This time his eye took in her swollen stomach. He started to rub his own belly silently in a slow, circular motion. As he rubbed, he thrust it out insolently, making what seemed to Jenny a grotesque parody of her pregnancy. Then abruptly, he stopped and pointed at Jenny's stomach, the laughter silently growing on his grinning face.

To Jenny, this was no innocent commenting in childlike muteness on the miracle of the forthcoming birth. This was as sinister as an invasion of the child in her womb. Something snapped in fear inside Jenny and she screamed.

"NO, never!!!" Throwing her canvas to one side, Jenny leapt up, a cornered female beast and rushed at him. She stumbled and fell face first down into the bracken. Unable to get up, she wailed loudly in fear and then mustered herself to her feet, ready to defend herself against her "enemy". He was nowhere to be seen. Sensing he must have disappeared behind the wall she had been painting, Jenny darted round the outside of it, only to come face to face with a large male Kudu antelope. For a moment, it stood there quivering, looking back at Jenny, then in a thudding of hooves, the great buck bounded off scudding through the undergrowth and bracken down the hill and out of sight and hearing. Weeping loudly, Jenny stumbled back towards the truck. She called for the dog but there was no sign nor sound of him anywhere.

"Butch! BUTCH! - Come here boy!" Frantic with fear, Jenny grabbed at her belongings, spilling the turpentine in the jar and scrambled into the cab. She tried the ignition. It wouldn't start. She was in a near panic as she tried it again. Still, it refused to catch.

"God help me!" she wailed as she saw through the windscreen the old man approaching, grinning wordlessly. Sobbing, Jenny tried the engine once more and this time it growled into life. Without a pause, just as the old fellow stepped round to her side of the cab, she threw the truck forwards in first gear accelerating all the while. Wildly, careless, she began her careering drive homewards to the safety of her husband's arms, not slowing even for the most dangerous corners in her descent from the mountain of madness she had just escaped.

Van had grease all over his hands. The valve from the old pump that fuelled the farm's needs for water and electricity from the little stream had been playing up. Taking out a rag from his back pocket, he wiped away most of the grease from the surface of his hands. Later, he would have to go across and see to the dipping of the sheep, to make sure Petros, his supervisor was carrying out his task properly. The dog brushing against his legs just at that moment gave Van a jolt. Breaking his concentration, he muttered.

"Hello Butch old Boy."

He was about to pick up a spanner to tighten the cap on the valve when he remembered that Butch had gone off with Jenny in the truck earlier.

"Where's Jenny, boy?" he asked of the dog. - Perhaps she had already come home but he hadn't heard her because he had been so engrossed. He better get back up to the house just in case she was worried about where he was. Putting down his tools, Van walked up the hill from the stream and scanned the driveway. There was no sign of the truck.

"Jesus," he muttered to himself. "I hope nothing's happened." In his mind, he had a picture of Jenny going off the road, or of her falling down and hurting herself and being unable to get up, perhaps even aborting. He started to walk up towards the main gate. Just then, he heard the sound of the pick-up and he sighed in relief. It was still very distant, but even then, he could detect that something was wrong. She was going much too fast. He stood waiting for her to turn into the driveway. He would have to rebuke her for driving so carelessly. He felt angry. Just then, she turned in and as she did, Van was awed at the speed at which she came racing towards him. It was almost as if she was bent on self destruction.

As the vehicle came to a crazy halt, Van walked swiftly over to the passenger door and opened it. Jenny fell into Van's arms weeping loudly and repeating his name over and over again.

"What's the matter, what's happened sweetheart?" Van asked in alarm. - "For Christ's sake, what is it girl?" - Van was more than disturbed by his wife's open hysteria.

"He wants my baby!"

It all seemed too much like a nightmare.

"Who wants your baby?" Van shook his wife. "Who are you talking about? Get a hold of yourself Jenny."

Through the tears, Jenny pleaded;

"You know - the old man the one who's always watching us!"

Instantly, Van knew whom it was that Jenny meant. His face grew grim and ashen as he wheeled towards the house. In an instant, he was back, walking towards the truck, loading the shotgun.

"No Van, you mustn't, please don't!" Jenny cried

out clinging to his arm. Van merely pushed her aside, out the way, and made for the truck door. He was about to climb in when Jenny flung herself on his arm again.

"No Van, NO!"

Van's eyes were bloodshot. He started and stared about like a madman, not hearing, not focusing. Then suddenly, he broke and fell onto the bonnet, his face in his hands, in tears. Jenny, weeping too, cast her arms around him, shaking and holding on to him with every breath in her body.

Very slowly, Van turned to her, his voice flat and cold.

"I swear to you Jenny, if that black bastard comes near you again, I'm going to blow his head off! - Let me call the police. He's crazy, dangerous. They can lock him up for life as far as I'm concerned!"

Jenny, pulling herself together, tried to appeal to reason.

"He mustn't get to us Van, we mustn't let him affect us like this."

Taking Van's face in both her hands, she leaned towards him and kissed him tenderly, pleading.

"Van," she said, "It doesn't matter about anything - as long as we have each other, as long as we can be together!"

Early the following day at the Inyanga Police Station, it was an ugly and angry Van Vuren that walked through the door to confront the local Inspector of Police. He shoved past a constable who was in the process of sorting out a domestic dispute that had erupted between a husband and wife the night before resulting in the husband getting hit over the head with an axe by his wife, angry at his unfaithfulness. Fortunately it had only glanced a blow that had caused him to see more red than reason. And now the handkerchief held up to his cut, he was screaming at his wife who returned his oaths doubly as he dealt them while the constable played piggy in the middle, taking the worst of it from both sides.

"Inspector Robson, he's in?!" Van more bawled than asked of the constable.

The constable, in between attempting to fill in a report on the alleged assault between the black couple, endeavoured to maintain the helpfulness for which a policeman's life was a friend of the people.

"Uh ... if you just hold on sir, I'll check and see if the Inspector is free."

"Don't worry, I'll see for myself," stated an angry and uncomprising Van Vuren, sweeping past the policeman, lifting the counter flap and storming through towards Inspector Robson's office at the back of the little police station. Sweeping the door open, Van marched in on the Inspector and demanded without even waiting for the Inspector to look up from his desk, as he slammed the door behind him;

"You better hear me out Robson, I'm bloody pissed off!"

"Van Vuren!" Robson looked up in surprise.

"Listen to me and listen good!" Van interjected, not wasting time with explanations or acknowledgements as he pulled a seat up right in front of the Inspector's desk. Leaning across the table he demanded.

"If that old black bastard harasses my wife or I once more, I'll sort him out for good!"

"Just a minute Van! - Whoa there! Start from the beginning. How can I help if I haven't the foggiest what you're talking about?"

Van realised he was getting a bit carried away and that he wasn't making much sense.

Small wonder since he himself had been so psyched up as a result of the occurrence and the sleepless night he had spent chewing it over or rather, it chewing over his mind as he tossed and turned on his pillow. So drawing a deep breath to calm himself, he began his story of how the old man had come into their lives, how he was always spying on them and of how the old man had threatened Jenny as he saw it in the last encounter with his wife. When he was through, he looked at Robson, waiting for action.

"Now, tell me again, this old bugger has been harassing you and your wife - threatening her you say?"

Van retorted angrily;

"I've already told you - you heard what I said!"

Placatingly, Robson tried to calm Van.

"Ease up now Van. The old guy, I know the one you mean - he doesn't speak, got some teeth missing so how could he have threatened you?"

Interrupting almost with a shout, Van interjected:

"That's the one! - You know about him then!"

"Sure we know about him Van. A bit eccentric. Maybe even slightly simple. Wanders around the hills at night. Regarded by the locals as a bit of a legend."

"Well, since you know whom I'm talking about, can't you go out and pick him up, put him away?!"

"Don't you see Van," said Robson quietly, "that he hasn't done anything, really."

"Hasn't done anything!" Van screamed. "He only

threatened my wife and child!"

Robson interposed;

"Well, I mean he didn't exactly say he was going to kill her, did he now? Look, can't you see Van that the old blighter is just a bit eccentric. I mean, he's totally bananas, I'm sure, but totally harmless too."

Van shook his head in total disbelief, incredulous that the Inspector could not understand nor see the threat the old man posed. Robson continued.

"You've got to realise that you'd make yourself slightly more than unpopular with the locals if word got around that you were responsible for having the old boy locked up."

Van reacted violently to this apparent casualness on the part of the police chief. Pushing his chair back and jumping to his feet, he shouted;

"If that bastard comes near me again, I swear to you, I swear I'll..."

"What'll you do Van? - Take the law into your own hands?"

Realising no help was forthcoming from the police, Van wheeled, spitting out the words in contempt before leaving the room.

"Thanks a lot for your help Inspector! - I'm sorry to have taken so much of your time."

He stormed out the office in a fury, banging the door loudly again behind him. The constable and husband and wife who were having the domestic paused from their debate to watch Van go.

In the farmhouse lounge, an old and weary Van Vuren rose to his feet from the dining room table and gazed at his hostages in the darkening room. Adjusting the shotgun under his arm, he grunted with a look of disgust at the couple slumped on the couch. Backing to the sideboard, he took the brandy bottle in his hand, lifted it to his mouth and drank the neat spirit. It was now nearly empty. Slowly, shotgun under his one arm, brandy bottle in the other hand, the old Van Vuren walked across to the Grahams. On the side table near the husband, he tentatively placed the brandy. Backing away, he commanded the man.

"You can drink!"

The husband took the bottle and instinctively wiped the top before swallowing. With the back of his hand, he wiped his mouth and was about to set the bottle back on the side table when Van interjected.

"What about the lady. Yes - you!" He barked as she looked up at him.

"Drink!" he commanded her. - Duly, the husband passed the brandy on and the wife took a gagging swig before handing it back to her husband to place on the coffee table next to him.

"Look old man," the husband began to stutter an apology, "we haven't done anything to harm you. Just let us go and we'll forget it, ok? I'm sorry I was so rude to you. I'm sorry for your hard luck!"

Van spun on the husband with a scream.

"Hard luck! - Is that what you call it! - You haven't learned a bloody thing, have you?"

Quickly, Van snatched the bottle from the table and backed away. Taking a last swallow, he flung it against the wall. It shattered loudly just as a clap of thunder rent the sky. The rain began to fall hard and heavy on the corrugations of the farmhouse roof.

Swinging the gun with both hands back and forwards over the husband and wife, Van started to

shiver and groan as if in pain.
"Just like the night Amanda was born."

In her hospital bed, Jenny shook from the last stages of her labour. Sweat ran from her face. Her hair was matted to her scalp. Her eyes rolled as if a wild animal in pain. Outside the hospital window, a storm was raging and Jenny's spasms came thick and fast between flashes of thunder and lightning. Sitting up, Jenny let out a scream, primitive as the heart of Africa itself and then collapsed back in a sweat onto the dripping pillow.
"A little girl, Mrs. Van Vuren," said the doctor, holding up a bawling bundle of red.
Jenny smiled wearily and closed her eyes, falling instantly into a deep, long sleep.

"You can open your eyes now!" Van's laughing voice shattered the hushed silence.
Jenny looked up to confront the biggest teddy bear she had ever seen. Van grinned widely, the proudest Dad in Christendom, beaming at his now six-month old daughter and his lovely wife on the settee. He had bought the gift from Umtali that very day. While Amanda breast fed on Jenny's lap, his wife looked up giggling, feasting her eyes on the fluffy toy.
"It's beautiful!"
Suddenly, her face took on a very serious expression, mock serious.
"No, wait a minute, it's not beautif ... it's ... it's HOGARTH! That's his name, Hogarth the huge; a daddy sized teddy so that daddy can hug him when mummy's not around."
Smiling, Van echoed Jenny:

"Hogarth, that's his name then. For when I get jealous of the two of you!"

Jenny pouted her lips obstinately.

"But I want him all for myself." Looking down at Amanda, she asked her daughter who was engrossed still in seeing what she could get from her mother's left teat.

"What do you say Amanda - can I have him all to myself as well as you and daddy?"

Just at that moment, full of milk, baby Amanda gave a little smile as she broke wind loudly with a belch that surprised even her mum. Jenny laughed.

"See, she says there's nothing wrong with being greedy." Then, reaching her hand out to Van, she held him and said:

"But I already have my daddy bear, don't I?"

"You've got me whether you like it or not my love", replied Van, bending down to kiss them both.

These were happy years for the Van Vurens: Amanda and the joy they shared brought them even closer together than ever before. They were, it seemed, the ideal family and the days passed unnumbered. The farm was running smoothly too, and Van was starting to show a real profit. They bought a new truck, and together, took it often for a picnic to their favourite spot where, in all probability, Amanda had been conceived. Inyangombi mountain pool. Jenny looked stunning, her healthy tan such a honeyed change from the pale white features of the English milkmaid that had first come to Africa and met Van in the bar at Troutbeck. One Sunday morning as usual, they went down to the pool and waterfall with the tartan rug and picnic basket. Amanda was now three years old. On the faithful tartan rug, Jenny spread a veritable feast. Quiche and cold barbecued chicken, apples fresh from the Inyanga orchards, fresh oven bread. Together, they went paddling down the stream that bled off into the pine forest. Jenny led the way, bottle of white wine in hand, to find a place to leave the wine to chill at the bottom of the stream. She was about to place the bottle between two rocks where the current would not roll it away when her daughter pointed to the leafy branch overhead.

"Look mummy, daddy, - thnake!"

Amanda's was a childhood lisp. But it made her irresistible, especially to grown men like Dawie who became completely childish himself when in her presence. He spoilt her rotten, always bringing chocolates and sweets, even when Jenny used to try and dissuade him. He even threatened to settle down and marry Sheila if she was not careful, just so he could become a father. All these things were the memories that made up the reel of those happy years together. And the incident of the snake in the tree.

"Look mummy, daddy - thnake!"

When Jenny did look up above her daughter's head, she saw the green creature sunning itself in an emerald coil above them and she let out a scream of fright dropping the bottle into the water. Van, just behind her, looked up and recognised it at once as an innocuous and totally non-malevolent Western Green Water Snake and started to laugh. Jenny was furious. "If it's not some dirty old guy spying on the Van Vuren family, it's a bloody snake now watching us!" She tried to run away but tripped or slipped on a stone covered with green slime in the bed of the stream and fell splashing into the water.

It was Amanda's humour, her laughter at seeing her mother making a big joke splashing about in the water that restored Jenny's own sense of humour. Soon the whole family was laughing, especially when Van pointed out that the snake was harmless.

"At least the wine's not broken," Jenny added.

"And thanks to Amanda, we've got a 'thnake' to look after it for us free of charge. Our personal wine guardian." Van retorted.

They all splashed each other getting their clothes fully soaked all the way back to the tartan rug on the edge of the pool and had a picnic they would never forget. And the wine was perfectly chilled, to toast their future together, having been guarded by "someone" they didn't even have to pay for the duty.

But Amanda was incorrigible. She kept discovering things like beetles and frogs and chameleons and besporting them in front of her nervous mother.

"Look Mummy, thpider!" she would boast, while a hairy and harmless baboon spider sat meek as a lamb on the palm of her hand, bringing the house down in shrieks from an hysterical Jenny Van Vuren.

One fine morning, Jenny was in the kitchen preparing lunch when Amanda walked up to her mother's turned back and tapped her on the shoulder quietly. When her mother glanced about to see what her daughter wanted, there on her outstretched and nonchalant hand was a spiny armadillo lizard.

"I found a wee cwocodile mummy!" came the seemingly innocent speech from the young girl. But Amanda knew that her mother was not quite as Africanised as herself, and her mother's cries of "Van, VAN! - Come here at once!" caused her to drop the lizard in fright. The little creature, equally alarmed with the gathering hysteria, scuttled to safety behind the paraffin fridge as Amanda's dad came strolling in, newspaper in hand.

"What's the matter love?" Van asked of Jenny.

Exasperated, Jenny sobbed;

"That daughter of yours keeps bringing bits of Africa into my house - live bits!" She accused pointing with her trembling hand, "like that lizard behind the fridge!"

Van Vuren couldn't help but smile at his wife's consternation, for she looked prettier than ever, the more flustered she became. He beamed at her, barely able to suppress his laughter. But he knew he mustn't give in to the amusement of the situation, or likely as not, he would be going without his dinner.

"That daughter of ours brings Africa into our house because she's curious, my darling. After all, she is intelligent, thanks to your brains, as well as being beautiful, again thanks to her mother's good looks. And, of course, she happens to be interested in life, not just in painting uninhabited ruins, because she is the daughter of one of Africa's most illustrious sheep farmers who has a particularly good eye for all creatures great and small, especially when they are able to produce little lambs like this one!"

Van couldn't keep it up any longer and he burst into laughter. Soon the whole family was shaking with proverbial jelly in their bellies as Van on his hands and knees, tried to extricate the unfortunate reptile from behind the fridge with his newspaper and words of encouragement.

"Nice lizard, good lizard, pretty Lizzie, come on, be good now, come on out of there, good lizzie!"

But it was in Amanda's fourth year that things began to turn sour. Lying in bed, Jenny turned to her husband one night, quietly confiding in him.

"Honey, I'm worried about Amanda. She's been losing an awful lot of weight lately. Tonight, she just couldn't keep her supper down I've even noticed that her hair is coming out when I brush it in the morning. She's lost nearly ten pounds in the last couple of weeks. I weighed her on the scales this evening."

Van reached out not saying much and took his wife's hand gently.

"Go on love..."

"Well, it's not that she's been complaining or anything. But well..."

"Tell me love."

"It's almost as if she's been trying extra hard to be happy, I know that sounds stupid."

"I think I know love. I've seen it myself. It's as if something was eating her up inside."

"But Van, she's too young to have any emotional worries. And we're a happy family, even if we do occasionally disagree."

"You'd better take her in to Dr Mitchell tomorrow in Umtali and ask him to get her referred to a specialist if necessary."

"That's what I want to do Van. God, I hope our darling is alright!"

Van tried to soothe his wife.

"I'm sure it's just a bug of some kind or other that children get. She said at supper that her tummy was sore. We'll see how she is tomorrow." Van leaned over and kissed his wife on the lips. Then he switched out the light.

A cloud of pain descended on the Van Vuren household. Jenny, at the dinner table, wept openly. Van was doing his best to try and comfort her. However, he too, was distracted and suffering.

"I'm sure it can't be as the doctor says!" Van spat out the words stubbornly. "The results of the tests must be wrong - she's five years old next month. God can't give cancer to a five year old!"

Smashing his fist on to the table, Van started to tremble violently. Jenny, through her tears, tried to explain to Van.

"Amanda has to go into the capital. That's the only place they can give her treatment. She needs transfusions regularly. And cobalt..."

Hysterically Jenny wails,

"Even if she lives, they say she'll never be off her treatment and she will never ever be able to have children!"

At a loss, Van wrings his hands, futile with the despair and inadequacy. After an age, Jenny puts her hand on his and looking in to Van's face tells him;

"Honey, I have to go with her to Salisbury. See? - I'll write. I'll phone every day and let you know how she is."

Getting up, a haggard Van Vuren walks over to the window. He turns abruptly and smashes his fist into the palm of his hand. Then he sits in a slump.

"Damn it! It's a bloody incurable curse on our lives! Why can't things go the way one wants them just once, are we never in control, God!"

It is some weeks later in the evening. Van, sprawled in an armchair, with a brandy bottle nearly empty beside him. Listlessly, automatically, he lifted the glass and drank. To anyone watching, it would have been apparent that the man had not shaved for several days. The phone rang and he jumped to his feet to answer it. Without waiting, he blurted out.

"How is she Jenny? Any improvement?"

Gradually, as he sat listening to his wife two hundred miles away in Salisbury, Van's shoulders began to sag and his face grew ashen. After a lengthy pause, he spoke in monotone.

"Alright, I know, I know. Listen, bring our baby back tomorrow. OK. Whenever you can, we'll handle it somehow, together." He started to cry openly into the mouthpiece. "Jenny, I need you."

Dropping the receiver, Van's head fell to his lap. He wept openly. The silence of the night was wracked by a grown man's painful sobs.

Petros, the supervisor, chased the sheep into the dip while his master, nearby, leant on a wall watching without interest.

Petros started work on the farm when Van first came to Inyanga. Together, they fought off dysentery and pulpy kidney, leopards, helped the ewes to give birth, built the pens, the farm house, and the sheep dip. Petros loved his life with his master who had seen to his son's education fees at Penhalonga Mission School. Yet Petros owed his first loyalty to his land, to Africa. And as he watched his master smash his fist repeatedly on the stone wall of the dip tank, Petros' black heart ached, knowing only one possible solution to this master's pain.

Slowly, he edged over to stand alongside Van Vuren, and then, almost in a whisper, he said to his master.

"Master Van. I sorry for your trouble. Maybe I help you Master Van."

Weakly, Van smiled at his labourer, knowing the compassion in the man.

"I doubt you can help Petros."

But Petros was insistent. He had something important to say, something that burned inside him.

"But Master Van," he tugged at his master's sleeve. "I help you make the piccanin better."

This encroachment on his pain was more than Van could bear. He wheeled on his employee, enraged.

"How the hell do you think you can help Petros? By bringing in a witchdoctor or something!"

Petros affirmed quietly:

"Yes, Master Van."

Van was distracted from this conversation by the arrival of the farm truck driven by Jenny. A pale and thin Amanda stared bleakly out of the passenger window, mustering a gaunt smile at seeing her father. Van walked over to meet his family and opening the door, lifted his daughter out and began to stroke her hair with infinite tenderness.

"How is my little angel?" He looked down at her. "Do you want to see the sheep having their bath honey?"

Amanda cast her eyes downward.

"Daddy, I'm sore."

Helplessly, her father tried to soothe his daughter's pain.

"Hush darling. We'll go back to the house and I'll read you your favourite story; Sleeping Beauty."

Looking up into her father's eyes with complete trust, Amanda asked the question that broke her father's heart and mind.

"Daddy, why isn't there a prince to kiss me and make it better when I go to sleep?"

This was more than Van could take. Barely, he held himself back from showing the intensity of his pain to his daughter. He placed her in the cab and turned away, tears welling in his eyes. Over his shoulder he called out to Jenny.

"I've ... I've just got to give Petros some instructions. Then we'll go home for the day."

As he walked heavily towards the dip, his heart was aching. On reaching the chief labourer, Van swallowed. He looked as if he was about to speak to him, but the words wouldn't come.

"You want something Master Van?" Petros enquired.

Slowly and deliberately, as if going against everything he had ever believed Van spoke.

"Petros?"

"Yes, Master Van?"

"I want you ... I want ... I want you to bring me this witch doctor."

Van glanced over his shoulder to ensure that Jenny was out of earshot. Petros shook his head.

"No, Master Van."

"What do you mean NO?" interjected Van angrily. "You said a witchdoctor could help."

Earnestly, Petros assured him;

"Yes, Master Van. My nanga can help. But he is very powerful, this nanga. And you must come and see him. He cannot come to your house Master Van..."

In a low urgent whisper, Van pressed.

"Alright Petros. Now listen. I want you to go and see

this doctor of yours and make an appointment with him. And I want you to come and take me to his house tonight."

"Yes, Master Van. I come tonight."

"You're not to speak to anyone about this Petros. Especially not to my wife."

"I understand Master Van."

Van wheeled and strode back to the truck where Jenny and Amanda were waiting. Climbing into the driver's seat, he started up the engine and turned back for the homestead, watched until out of sight by his chief labourer. Then, turning to the man next to him, Petros barked an order. Without waiting to see if it was acknowledged, he began to run across the meadow towards the mountainside.

At the dinner table that night, when Amanda was asleep, Van sat opposite his wife with his food. He had no appetite. He looked down at his plate, refusing to meet his wife's searching look.

"Why aren't you trying to eat Van? - It doesn't help to have two sick people around the house."

"I've got to go out later Jenny. Some of my new ewes are expecting and I want to make sure everything is ok."

"We've got to be happy for Amanda's sake darling," Jenny said, misconstruing her husband's lack of appetite. "We've got to make her time with us as worthwhile as is humanly possible."

Van echoed her words flatly; "As humanly possible."

"Well, that's all we really have, don't we? Other than each other. Do you really have to go out tonight?" Jenny pleaded, reaching for Van's hand.

Van barked back "Yes!"

Jenny, not knowing the real reasons for Van's reactions, apologised.

"I'm sorry Van. I know that the farm has to keep running."

Just then, there was a knock at the door. Van instinctively jumped up to his feet and rushed over to answer it.

"I'll get it."

His wife watched him cross the room and open the door. She sensed that something was not quite in place. But she couldn't know exactly what it was that was troubling her. She watched Van say a few words sotto voce to someone. Then quietly, she watched him walk back towards her at the table.

In answer to her questioning look, Van commented; "It's Petros. I've got to go now."

He started to make for the door, only to turn back in his tracks and came over to Jenny, leaning down to kiss her tenderly.

"I love you Jenny Van Vuren."

"And I love you Van, more than I can say."

Then Van exited, closing the door behind him. Jenny sat blankly while she listened to the pick-up's engine throb into life. Unmoving, she gazed at the door until the sound of the truck disappeared into the night.

Inside the cab, Van, with his eyes fixed emotionlessly on the road, barked at Petros next to him.

"Where to?"

"Just up the road baas."

In silence they drove for another few minutes until Petros interrupted Van.

"Stop here baas."

Pulling over to the side of the road, Van switched off the ignition. Together, they climbed out and stood at the foot of the mountainside in the cold moonlight. Van switched on a torch, and led by his labourer, the two men began to climb the hill. Around them, through the grass and heath, the wind blew its hushed voice across the land. The damp of the night dew hung heavily in the air. After several minutes, the sound of their belaboured breathing could be heard mingling with the wind, the only evidence of life in the night. The slope suddenly steepened into a rock face made up of large and awkward-to-negotiate granite boulders. Van grasped at bunches of knot grass and shrubs to keep his balance. In spite of the sweat he had worked up on the ascent, he shivered inside. Just at that moment, his torch picked up the entrance to a cave in the rocks. A low entrance into which a man must stoop.

"This is the place Petros?"

"This is the place, Master Van."

For some moments, Van stood in the mouth of the cave as if undecided to go on. Then he bent his neck and stepped into the darkness, darkness so thick as almost to be tangible. Unannounced, a wood fire inside the cave flared into life with a crackle of energy. It illuminated Van's face as his eyes widened in shock and disbelief.

"You ... you!"

He could hardly believe or credit who it was in front of him, squatting behind the flames, bare from the midriff up except for a string of vertebrae and ritual beads around his neck. The old man's eyes were closed and he made not a motion or indication that Van was present in the cave.

Without warning, it seemed to Van that a voice was heard, a disembodied thing, deep and resonant, coming at him from the back of the cave. Van's first instinct was to block his ears, for the voice seemed to be coming from inside his head.

"Most people call mc the silent one!"

Stumbling on his feet, Van tried to find something to say, anything, and something to hold on to, for it was as if he was losing his mind. The voice rang out in his ears once again.

"You may sit."

Overwhelmed by something stronger than himself, an authority unknown to him, Van slumped into a squat on the ground. And again the voice:

"You still do not know me, even though you think you know my face."

The old man's eyes opened. In them, the flames leapt and danced their reflections. He began to rock backwards and forwards, laughing silently. Like a tide, the voice rolled in with its deep, unstoppable thunder.

"You have considered me as your enemy yet now you want me to heal the child."

Their eyes met. Van was agog, stunned, out of his depth. As the old man watched him, he felt powerless to lift a hand. He felt the fear percolate deep into the marrow of his being.

"You owe it to me; you owe it to me because you do not understand. Yes, I see you. And I see you do not understand, even when you choose to see me."

Van found himself lost in this tide that defied the borders of time and experience.

"When I saw you with the child close to the earth's mouth, I said I would heal her."

Faintly, inside his being, Van felt a moment's hope, a slight surge as he sought to find his reason. Forcing himself to speak, Van spluttered:

"But ... I... you saw me?"

Once again, he was overwhelmed by something stronger than reason.

"I saw you. I hear you. Do you think you are alone in my world? Even the stones have eyes."

Suddenly, the voice became abrupt, chilling.

"Then this is what I want in return. To show you have not forgotten what you owe me, one year from tomorrow night, you will bring me your child, to see me."

To Van's mind, the spectre of the witchdoctor claiming Amanda was more than he could vindicate. In his very instincts, a rage rose up from his depths. He heard his own voice cry out blood red;

"No! Never!"

"You want your child to live?" came back the annihilating reply.

Again, Van was swamped, out of his depth, lost.

"Yes" he whispered in submission, helplessly.

There was a pause as the ancient one let the import sink in. But in Van's unconscious depths, he heard himself affirm his will to not honour his commitment to the man. He heard himself cry out: "No, never!"

Instead, his voice responded;

"Anything... anything you say."

The nanga gave his command.

"Tomorrow, you will meet me at the setting of the sun."

Van could only whisper or utter a single word, for he needed this power, this unknown and supernatural hope at any cost.

"Where?" Van said.

"By the old stones where your wife met me. On the hill. You know the place. You will bring the child."

In his mind, Van saw a picture of the old fort in the last rays of the setting sun.

"Yes," he conceded helplessly.

The voice spoke once more.

"You may go now," and Van felt himself released as if from iron bonds. Stumbling to his feet, he backed out of the cave in a run. Shuddering violently, the sound of an old man's laughter seemed to follow him into the night, echoing round the walls of darkness in his mind.

Jenny was waiting back at the farmhouse. For some reason, she felt afraid for Van and was unable to sleep. The door was open to the night as she listened for the sound of the truck. When she finally heard it approaching, she rushed outside to greet her husband. As Van got out of the vehicle, Jenny hugged him tightly.

"Oh Van, I was so scared! I couldn't sleep. I don't know why?"

Van rigidly asked Jenny how Amanda was.

"She's sleeping," Jenny replied.

"Let's also go and get some sleep. I'm tired too," was all that Van could say. He led the way inside the farmhouse in front of Jenny and bolted the door behind them. Jenny did not ask why her man was so far away, but saw rather the weariness written deep into his features. In bed together, the moonlight through the curtains shone onto their faces. Jenny turned away and closed her eyes while Van lay on his back staring upwards at the ceiling blankly. The events of the evening spun through his head accusingly. He heard the voice come echoing back in again;

"One year from tomorrow night, you will bring me your child."

He heard his own voice deep inside shouting back - "NO, never!" And Jenny's voice joined in solidarity with his own... "NO, never!"

Exhausted, Van closed his eyes, but the laughter seemed to penetrate his brain like the wind through the eaves of the roof. It ran like an echo round his mind, could not be excluded or cut out. A river in flood from an old man's toothless mouth.

Van woke with a start, the morning sunlight streaming onto the disheveled blankets about him. Sitting up, he shook Jenny urgently.

"What day is it - what is the date?"

Startled from sleep, Jenny fumbled to grasp what Van wanted.

"Wh...What?"

"What is the DATE Jenny?" Van insisted.

"Uh, it ... it's the .. 29th February 1960." Jenny mumbled.

"You sure?!" Van cried aloud. Suddenly, he began to roar with laughter waking Jenny open-eyed with shock.

"What's the matter? Have you gone mad?"

Van continued to shake with laughter. After a while he spluttered loudly.

"It's a leap year! For Christ's sake, next year - 1961 - there is no twenty-ninth of February!"

"You find that funny?" Jenny enquired of Van earnestly, incredulously. "Get a hold of yourself Van,

you'll frighten Amanda if she sees you like this."
At the mention of her name, Amanda appeared in the doorway, woken by her father's hysteria. She looked emaciated, pale.

"Daddy?" She asked uncertainly.

Still laughing, Van Vuren climbed out of bed and held out his arms to his daughter.

"Don't worry honey - Daddy loves you - you're the best little girl in the whole world and your Daddy loves you and your Mummy so-oo much!"

Van could not suppress himself. The laughter boomed out of him. Very soon, Jenny started to become infected by this new lease of life in her husband.

"How much is so-oo much?" Jenny asked giggling.

"So-oooooo much!!!" Van reiterated, wobbling his jowls with the vowels of what he was saying and spreading his arms as wide as he could while waving and jiggling his hands. Laughing, he collapsed in a heap onto the bed on top of his wife. Soon, the whole family were shaking with laughter in bed together, rocking and hugging one another, happier than they had been in a long, long while.

Amanda lay between her parents, her pain temporarily forgotten. Her father turned to her, brushing the hair back from her forehead.

"Tonight, my little princess, I'm taking you to a castle way up there..." Van smiled at his daughter, his arm sweeping to the view of the mountains outside the window,

"What are you going on about," Jenny asked with a smile. "I truly do think you've gone stark raving mad!"

Van's face took on an earnest expression. He paused for a moment before commenting in a low voice.

"No, I'm not the one who's crazy." Then, turning it into a joke, he added;

"Admittedly, strange things do happen to me when it is a full moon, as well as on leap years, but what the heck?!" And he started to laugh loudly, though somewhat forced this time. Abruptly, he jumped out of bed and called out as he left the bedroom.

"I've just got to make one phone call before I forget. I'll be back in a moment, so you two, keep the bed warm for me."

On the telephone, Van spoke insistently to his friend Dawie in a hushed voice lest he be overheard.

"Yes, that's right! - I want you to invite Jenny later, for late tea - supper - about four-thirty, five. No, it's a surprise. Actually, I think she needs a break, to get out of herself. Yah, see if you can cheer her up, you know...That's right." Again a forced laugh from Van before the conversation continued. "Yes, if you call her just after breakfast - but make sure that she comes, ok? Thanks Dawie, you're a great friend and I mean it...Ya, I appreciate it... Bye for now!"

The goodwill of the morning still prevailed at the breakfast table. It shone into the house with the morning sun. It was in the colour of the bacon and eggs. It sweetened the coffee. Everyone, including Amanda, ate heartily. When the phone rang. Jenny jumped up to her feet.

"I'll get it!'

Van smiled as he watched her walk across to the little table and pick up the receiver.

"Oh, hello Dawie."

She winked at her husband while she listened to Dawie on the other end, "Tonight? - No, I don't think so Dawie ... you know, Amanda."

At this Van interjected.

"What's Dawie say?"

Covering the mouthpiece, Jenny whispered loudly;

"He wants me to go over for dinner tonight. Says it's a surprise."

"Well, go Jenny." Van volunteered firmly. "As your husband, I'm ordering you to go - I'll look after Amanda!"

Somewhat hesitantly, Jenny took her hand off the mouthpiece.

"Alright Dawie, I'll come. About five o'clock. But I can't stay too late you understand ... yes," She giggled; "Van'll get jealous. Bye then, see you later."

Replacing the receiver on the hook, Jenny walked back to the breakfast table with a smile.

"A surprise? - I wonder what mischief that joker's got in mind for tonight?"

It was late afternoon at the Van Vuren's. Jenny came out of the bathroom having just put the finishing touches to her make-up.

"Look alright?" she asked Van.

"Too good for Dawie - that's for sure!" Van jibed.

"You sure everything will be fine with Amanda honey?"

"Everything will be just fine," Van assured his wife with a smile, "I promise." - And so saying Van held out the truck keys to her and as she came forward to take them, he caught her in his arms and kissed her slowly.

"Van, you've just messed my lipstick, you blighter!" Jenny giggled.

Pushing her out the house, Van watched until the

truck disappeared from view. Then he turned and went in to Amanda's bedroom. She was lying in bed, reading quietly. As her father came in, she looked up at him inquiringly.

"Where did mummy go?"

"She's gone to uncle Dawie's for supper honey," her Dad assured her. "Come on Sleeping Beauty ... time to get up. Do you remember that castle I promised to show you - well, we're going there now, just as soon as you've put on your jersey." He held out his arms to his daughter and helped her on with the cardigan. Then he said;

"Climb aboard, piggy-back time," and lifted her onto his shoulders. Amanda squealed and giggled delightedly.

"Mind your head," Van warned as they ducked out of the door of the house into the early evening air.

The figure of Van silhouetted against the setting sun as he ran up the side of the mountain towards the old fort, with his daughter on his back, made a primitive and myth-like double-headed giant. But Van was feeling strong, the hope beating inside him. At the first stone walls, Van took his daughter off his shoulders and deposited her lightly onto the ground. They walked forward, father and daughter, hand in hand, into the twilight. Soon, the figure of an old man came forwards, out of the stones towards them to greet them; the keeper of the stones of history.

Into the central enclosure of the ruins they walked together, to where the play was to be enacted. The old man lit a fire and the spreading flames danced in the red hues of sunset. The old man behind the dancing flames and behind him, Amanda lying on a plinth of stone. Sleeping Beauty in miniature, virginal on the sacrificial altar of an event older than time itself.

The silent one began to sway back and forth, and from his mouth came the low sound of a chant, soft as a prayer.

Van felt the hair on the back of his head begin to move. And sweat started to build in beads on his forehead. His eyes were fixed on the figure swaying behind the fire as he watched the ancient eyes of the silent one roll and close, seeking into a dimension beyond Van's grasp. As the last rays of the sun disappeared behind the horizon, the incantation grew in strength, slowly rolling in like an ocean.

Dropping some powder into a clay vessel on the fire, the witchdoctor began to change his voice, to alternate it as a reed solitary in the wind, a peculiar thin and haunting sound that reached to the very spine of Van's being. Stirring the liquid in the pot, the old man lifted it and handed it over the flames to Van to indicate that he should drink. Van felt the sweat slide heavily down his temples. Taking hold of the vessel in trembling hands, he took a long, deep draught.

It started slowly at first, the sound of the drums in his temples. The chanting of the dark figure in front of him seemed to get louder until it washed like a sea over him. He felt his body sway. Unannounced, the vision of an army of ghostly warriors rose from the stones around, joining in the chant and astounding his senses. Dressed in skins and masks, he saw them raise a phalanx of spears in a rattle into the air. He heard the spears being raised and then come thudding down into the ground, being raised again and come thudding down. The beat of the drums and voice of the chant got louder, louder. Van's head swam. The flames seemed to engulf him. He was sweating profusely as the world span before him and just before the whole universe turned into darkness, he recognised the toothless smiling face before him from a dream of long ago.

"Daddy, daddy, wake up!"

Van heard a voice deep in his subconscious. It was a voice that he knew he should know, should recognise. He felt himself rise from out of a dark cave, slowly, like a man from the grave. Opening his eyes, he was dazzled by the blinding glare of a sun white as creation. It stunned him, causing him to shelter from its holiness with an upraised hand across his face. Through his fingers, he recognised the face of an angel smiling.

"Amanda!" Van cried. "You're alright!"

Sitting up, Van gazed around him. There was no sign or trace of what had taken place the night before. It was just as if it all had been a long, bad dream. Except they were together, father and daughter, on the mountainside. The world was alive and the orange and red aloes glowed brightly beneath a blue sky of a new day.

The stone slab he had been lying on seemed familiar. Then he looked at his daughter smiling at him and the mist vanished. He called to her.

"Come on Amanda. We'd better get home or your Mummy will be worried."

Sliding off the stone, Van lifted Amanda on to it. Offering his shoulders to her, he said;

"Come on, climb aboard."

"No thank you Daddy, I want to walk."

Van was amazed at this unheard of request. He was

even more stunned when Amanda lightly jumped to the ground from some four feet up. She took his hand.

"Come on Daddy, Mummy will be worried."

Together, father and child began walking down the mountain into the morning, hand in hand away from yesterday's ruins.

Inside the farmhouse, a group of very troubled citizens were gathered. Inspector Robson was standing next to Dawie and his girlfriend trying to comfort a hysterical Jenny Van Vuren.

"God! - I don't know. I don't understand it." Jenny shrieked at Dawie. "Why did you let him do it!"

It was a very subdued Dawie who tried to mutter an apology uselessly.

"How was I to know Jenny? - I believed him. He said you needed a break and I believed him!"

At that moment, Amanda ran in through the open door closely followed by her laughing father. Dawie wheeled on Van, angry, hurt and indignant.

"What the hell do you think you're playing at Van Vuren?" Jenny burst into sobs as she rushed over and fell on her knees to comfort her daughter. Embracing her, she repeated over and over;

"My poor darling, my sweet!"

"It's all right Mummy, Daddy took me to the castle. He promised me!"

Turning to her husband, Jenny shrieked at him like an enraged and wounded beast.

"What the hell have you done Van? - Our daughter, our child is dying and you take her out all night. You're insane! - You ought to be locked away for life!"

Her outrage was interrupted by Amanda.

"No, it's alright Mummy... I'm better - see?"
So saying, the little girl does a somersault on the carpet. Jenny's system just could not take the shock. She fainted, caught just in time by Inspector Robson.

Some days later, Amanda was sitting playing with the dog, Butch, on the lounge floor, She was laughing wildly with energy and excitement as she rolled about. At the dining room table, Jenny looked on in amazement. She turned to face her husband, eyes wide open, voice hushed and serious.

"I don't believe it ... I ... just ... can't ... believe it!"
Van beamed back at her.

"You heard what the doctor said. He can't understand it himself. There's no apparent reason. He said that sometimes, the white blood cells can fight it off and occasionally, the disease can be turned around. But we still have to take her for regular check-ups."

Van reached out and took his wife by the hand.

"Just don't ask questions. Please Jenny, don't ask, and just accept it as the miracle it is."

"Give me a cigarette!" Jenny demanded of her husband, holding out a trembling hand.

"But you don't smoke!"

"I need a cigarette." She took it and drew in, inhaling the comforting smoke. Then burst out gagging, coughing and spluttering as she immediately proceeded to stub it out.

"Perhaps it's a drink that I need Van!" Suddenly she began to laugh.

"OK - OK. You don't have to tell me," she continued. "But just answer me this one question."

"What?" Van enquired furtively.

Getting up, Jenny left the room and returned with her handbag. She sat down again and opened the bag taking out a medicinal pouch of the sort that witchdoctors use.

"Van," she said, holding it out before his widening eyes, "Van, by any chance, did that old man perhaps have anything to do with all this?"

The night set in wildly in High Country. An old and bug-eyed Van Vuren paused from his memories and faced his hostage Graham.

"Give me a cigarette," he demanded, motioning with his shotgun.

"I don't smoke," said the young man seated next to his weeping wife on the settee of the farmhouse lounge.

"Hell!" muttered Van Vuren. He began to stomp around the room, restless as a caged lion. Behind him the husband began to move. Van wheeled on him with the gun.

"I have eyes in the back of my head now! - You see, I learnt my lesson in the end ... in the end."

An old and battle-worn Van Vuren began to weep.

"That's right, just when I thought I had him beaten. We even went away on holiday to celebrate, to Kariba Dam. We called it our second honeymoon."

Van remembered the first day of that holiday as if it was the very moment he was living in the present. It was the twenty-second of April, 1960. The weather perfect over the waters of Lake Kariba. In a motor boat on the lake, a happy and healthy Amanda trailed her hand over the side. Jenny shouted above the noise of the engine as her husband negotiated behind the wheel.

"I never realised how lovely the Lake is. It's almost like a sea."

"Yes, it is good to have got away!" Van bellowed back.

Diving into the cold bag, Jenny pulled out a beer and opened it.

"Want one?"

"Can I have some beer too Daddy?" asked Amanda. Van laughed.

"Only a sip now. Beer is definitely not for charming little princesses."

Leaning across the boat, he passed his daughter the open bottle and she duly took a sip before politely handing it back to her father. Suddenly, Amanda pointed to a skier in tow on the lake as they rocked across the wake of a motorboat going in the opposite direction.

"Look Daddy, Mummy, someone running on water!"

Through the laughter, Van was carried further into his memories of that Kariba holiday, to their first visit to a crocodile farm. In the background, the three of them could see a man with a small crocodile held firmly in his grasp, giving a lecture of epic proportions to the astounded tourists milling round. Jenny turned to him, prodding him with a laugh.

"Remember Manda's wee cwocodile in the kitchen?"

"She won't even go near a grasshopper now!" Van laughed back. "She's becoming a pwoper little lady, just like her English mamma."

And back at the hotel where they were staying, Van watched Amanda paddling and splashing about with a friend in the baby pool. A boy of about the same age. He watched her take his hand and lead him up the bank. Her body was no longer pale. It was Jenny that turned to her husband whose eyes were fixed in wonder on the beauty of their daughter.

"Happy darling?"

Van blinked dreamily at Jenny. Nodded in affirmation and asked her the same question.

"And you?"

Putting her finger to her lips, she motioned for silence, then whispered one word.

"Unspeakably!"

And Van remembered the hotel bedroom at night when Amanda was asleep. The softness of Jenny's lips and thighs. Their slow kisses and falling asleep in each other's arms. That holiday had passed too quickly. But the farm could not be left unattended forever.

However, they made a point of taking time to picnic together regularly at Inyangombi pool or down by the sheep pastures at lunchtime, Jenny bringing Van respite, food and drink to break the monotony of his day as well as bringing his daughter to him. Once they had a picnic on the grass on the old rug and Amanda, now a full five years old, hid her hands behind her back as her father approached. As Van drew near, she produced from behind her a motley assortment of daisies and sorrel leaves bunched in her little palm.

"Daddy, I picked you some flowers."

"Thank you my sweet," her father kissed her flopping down onto the blanket next to her and Jenny. Then rolling onto his back, with a sweep, he caught his daughter up in his arms and held her above him in the air as she kicked and squealed with delight. It was a picnic where the farm work was put off for the rest of the day and everyone went home and told stories and drank cocoa and ate biscuits and cake until they were too full to leave any room for supper. And nobody felt the slightest bit guilty, because being together made up for all the work that still needed to be done that day on the farm.

The first time Jenny had shown an interest in African artifacts and curios had given Van quite a start. She had gone to Inyanga village to do some grocery shopping and Van was reading quietly seated in his favourite chair when the door opened. Had it not been for the one squeaking hinge that he had been promising to oil into silence someday soon, he would not have looked up at all. But on hearing the door, he gazed up automatically and found himself staring into the grinning gargoyle face of some primitive demon made of wood that growled at him noisily.

"Hoi!" He exclaimed in fright.

The mask came away the reveal the laughing face of Jenny Van Vuren.

"How do you like it?" she giggled.

"I prefer your own face," Van admitted honestly.

"I've decided to make a collection. Come and see the carvings I've got in the boot. And you can help me unload them and carry them inside."

Van got up rather dubious about this sudden interest of Jenny's and it did take him some getting used to, all these bits and pieces of "primitive" art. Nevertheless, as it was something that Jenny had taken to, he accommodated accordingly, affording space for the new guests that were to live under his roof; soap stone carvings and statuettes and shields and masks, fly whisks and spears.

Jenny took some photographs of Amanda holding a young lamb dangling from her arms. The lamb looked huge for such a little girl. But it was the look on Amanda's face, of absolute divine adoration that had started the painting for Jenny. A painting of a young girl against a background of mountains, sunlight like a halo round her head, backlighting her gold hair. While Jenny was involved in doing the painting, she made Van and Amanda promise to stay away and leave her at it.

"I want it to be a real surprise. And beside, I don't want any criticism or peeking until it's finished."

One day, she called her husband out of the house where she was working in the sunlight.

"Van, it's ready."

Van walked across to admire her work, but what he saw was better than anything Jenny had ever done before. Van had never seen a painting so good in his life, even if he was biased and it was done by his wife. He tried not to sound too enthusiastic at first in case Jenny would think he was joking.

"Mmmm," he said, in between puffs of his pipe. "Yes, yes definitely. It's good Jenny, it's damn good, extraordinarily good, but of course, I could be mistaken. Perhaps the subject of the painting should come and give us her opinion on her mother's work." Jenny turned before Van could move out of the way and dabbed some paint on the end of his nose.

"Just watch this, Mr Van Vuren," she announced commandingly.

With a final flourish, she signed it; 'J. Van V. - 1/3/61'.

"There, I'm going to take it and get it framed this afternoon in Umtali. Promise me Van, that we'll hang it where everyone can see it when they come into the house. - I know I'm a show-off," she giggled, "but it's the best thing I've ever done."

Van hammed seriousness. He shook his head vehemently, rubbing his chin in his hand, an art critic in caricature.

"No, I'm afraid not Mrs. Van Vuren, we can't accept it. It'll have to go direct to the Tate Gallery, you see, the master of the house needs to sell it to make some money for the farm. -Well, let's see, maybe, just this once, we could accept it. Yes. I think so, an original J Van Vuren."

Together, they broke into laughter, throwing their arms around one another. Simultaneously, they looked at the painting again and Van shouted into the house;

"Amanda, Amanda! - Come and see the surprise your Mummy has for you!"

Amanda came running out and Van put his hands over her eyes.

"You're not allowed to peek now until I tell you."

He led her to the painting. Jenny was hushed. Then he counted loudly "one, two, three," and wiped his hands away to leave Amanda to gaze on the mirror of her soul. The little girl stood in silence and began to blush and look away, back to the painting and then to look away again and then back to it once more with an irrepressible giggle of wonder bubbling out from her enchanted heart.

Quietly, Van took Jenny's hand behind their daughter's back, and pulling her across to him with all the joy of first love trembling beneath the skin, he kissed her secretly while their daughter gazed and gazed and gazed at her mother's masterpiece.

The clock said nine and Jenny was still not back from Umtali. Van was worried. He felt something was wrong. Going over to the phone, he dialed Dawie's number to see, if by any chance, Jenny had dropped by to show him her completed painting. There was no reply from Dawie's. He'd probably gone out.

A knock at the door made Van spin around. With a sense of foreboding, he went across to answer it. He opened the door to face Inspector Robson in uniform, cap in one hand and the painting hanging loosely in his other. In slow motion, he watched the Inspector open his mouth slackly and mumble his name.

The scream came from deep within him.

"No! For Christ's sake NO!"

Inspector Robson's mouth was moving although the words he spoke somehow didn't really register.

"She must have swerved to avoid something ... the rain ... the road was slippery ... she ... she went over the edge ... Van I took the liberty of bringing Dawie with me."

A sheepish Dawie poked his head around the door hopelessly. He couldn't look at Van directly, but Van was anyhow oblivious of his presence. Van felt the tears spring hot into his eyes. He choked out the words.

"I don't believe it. Let me see - I want to see!" Summoning up his courage, his friend intervened.

"Van, you shouldn't. I'll take care of everything." Blinded by pain, Van cried out;

"For Christ's sake - I have the right!"

Inspector Robson placed his hand on Van's

shoulder.

"Dawie will stay with you tonight, you can go in the morning."

Van retaliated with a primeval cry, knocking Robson's hand out the way.

"NOW!!!"

The three men scrambled down the side of the hill towards the wreck. The night was very quiet but interspersed with flashes of lightning and rumbles of thunder promising more rain.

Twisted against a boulder at the bottom, the wreck lay motionless. On getting to it, Van moved as if in a dream. His torch shone on the back wheel. He moved it slowly across the bodywork. Observing the twisted shapes of the metal like faces caught in mid-scream, the shadows lay cut out of his own mind, missing words lost in the darkness. Slowly, he followed the light of the torch to the cab and through the tortured gap where the windscreen had been. On the rear view mirror inside, he noticed something dangling that he felt he had never seen before. It swung in the night wind backwards and forwards. Quickly, reaching his hand into the cab, Van caught the object and pulled it off past the steering wheel.

He knew what the object was even before he shone his torch onto the pouch lying cradled in his palm. The same witchdoctor's pouch given to Jenny when she was pregnant.

"My Christ!" Van oathed in the darkness, smashing his clenched fist into the side of the wreck. A clap of thunder and the rain began to fall.

Van sat numbly at the dining table fingering the pouch. Dawie sat wordlessly opposite him. It was as if

Van was obsessed, for he kept on twisting and turning the pouch on its thong about his fingers. Dawie broke the silence.

"Amanda's gone to sleep now."

Van paid no attention but kept turning the object over and over in his hand. Abruptly, he looked up at Dawie and said;

"Dawie, go home. I need to be alone."

"You sure Van?" Dawie asked uncertainly. Numbly, Van reiterated.

"Yes, Go!"

Hesitantly, Dawie got up to leave. Before he went out, he looked back at Van as if for reassurance. But Van was engrossed in the pain of his thoughts, twisting the pouch about in his fingers. And he carried on doing so until after the sound of Dawie's vehicle had driven off. Then he stood up and threw the pouch down on the table, walked over to the mantelpiece and lifted the shotgun off the wall. Loading it, he left the house, out into the night rain.

Van headed for the mountain, for the cave. He had but one thought, one purpose, and it drive him fast through the storm up the mountainside. He could taste the bile and blood in his mouth from over-exertion. He panted as he stood in the mouth of the cave. Breathlessly, he called out.

"You there, you fucking bastard?!"

Inside the cave there was silence. Only the noise of the driving rain outside. Silhouetted in a flash of lightning, Van stood in the entrance, he shouted again, his scream echoing around the walls.

"Come on out, you murdering bastard!"

There was no response. Then, as Van stepped in, without warning, a terrible leonine roar shattered the night. The leopard came arching up at him from the mouth of darkness, fangs bared, claws ready.

Instinctively, Van raised the gun and fired. He felt the weight of the creature knock into him and he fell.

After an age, Van stirred. The body of the beast lay heavily on top of him. His side had been clawed by the dying cat. His head was bleeding from where he fell. Beneath him, down in the valley, Van heard the long, slow howl of a dog.

Levering himself from underneath the leopard's body, Van scrambled to his feet.

"Christ, oh God, no, please, no!"

He started to run and stumble in a blind descent down the mountainside.

"Amanda! - AMANDA!"

Staggering, he fell breathlessly into the house through the open, swinging door on its crazy hinge. He slipped or rather tripped over something inert and landed face down in a puddle of rain on the floor. Lurching to his feet, his dog lay motionless before him, not breathing. Next, he staggered through to the bedroom, Amanda's bedroom, and switched on the light.

The blankets were pulled back. Amanda was gone. No sign nor sound. Just the door swinging on an un-oiled hinge, back and forth, like a ghost. On Van's face there came a look of pure terror. Why had he abandoned his daughter without thinking? - Rain swept in through the open window in a puddle on the floor. Instinctively, he realized it was too late. Van collapsed weeping onto the carpet, all strength gone out of him in a flood of realisation that he should never have left her alone. His sobs wracked the empty room as the wind blew in behind him.

In Van Vuren's lounge, the old Van Vuren walked slowly across to the table and slumped in a chair.

"They said it was just shock at finding herself alone that did it. That made her wander off into the night. But I knew better."

Suddenly, older than ever, Van sagged. Dropping the gun on the table top, his face fell into his hands and he began to weep.

His hostage, Graham, used the opportunity well. He sprang across the room and seized the weapon, turning it on Van Vuren. Swinging his arms wildly, Van screamed.

"Go away!"

There was a roar of flame followed by Van Vuren's body jumping backwards off the chair. He lay on the floor and writhed a while as a flower blossomed instantly, redly, across his chest.

Graham's wife began to wail, hysterical. Graham dropped the gun and ran over to his wife, pulling her to her feet.

"Let's get out of this madhouse!"

Pulling his wife through the door, they left, running towards the car in the rain. Inside the silent house, the wall clock began to chime the midnight in. The car spun off in a scream of wheels and headed away from the nightmare to a more familiar world.

Nearing the crest of the hill, the figure of an old man stepped into the headlights. He was bare from the waist and laughing toothlessly. Graham swerved and veered frantically as a woman's scream rent the night and the car left the road to plunge nearly a thousand feet into the valley below.

Early the next day, a hand replaced a blanket over a body lying alongside the red wreck. The hand belonged to Inspector Robson. Turning to the constable at his side, Robson ordered;

"Right, constable, take down this report... February 29th, 1988. One red sports car. Make - Mercedes sports ... Driver, European Male, early thirties. No other occupants. Probably swerved to miss a buck."

Overhead, the black eagle glided, climbing on the warm morning air. It turned its head and looked down on a police land rover on the road and observed the sun glinting off the remains of a red sports car far below. Climbing higher, the bird's eyes took in the horizon where the mountains, purple in the distance, led into a far country. The sun warmed its back and wings. The air blew past its pinions, a rushing, mighty wind.

This was the way the mountains had always been. This was the way of the eagle in the sky.

"Chisingaperi Chinoshura"

(A thing without end is mysterious.)

\- Shona Proverb.

www.ingramcontent.com/pod-product-compliance
Ingram Content Group UK Ltd.
Pitfield, Milton Keynes, MK11 3LW, UK
UKHW020219250726
13967UKWH00001B/79

9 781291 652277